Time for a Change

I walked down the hallway. Ahead of me, I saw Vanessa. Her black chiffon skirt swayed gently as she moved.

For the first time in my life, my cheerleading uniform didn't seem like the greatest outfit in the world. Suddenly it made me feel big and clunky.

That's when I realized I was sick of being plain old Patti Richardson. Right then I would have given anything to be dressed in a gauzy, floaty black skirt. Just like Vanessa.

The Paxton Cheerleaders

Go For It, Patti!
Three Cheers For You, Cassie!
Winning Isn't Everything, Lauren!
We Did It, Tara!
We're in This Together, Patti!

Available from MINSTREL Books

We're In This Together, Patti!

Katy Hall

A Parachute Press Book

PUBLISHED BY POCKET BOOKS

New York London Toronto Sydney Tokyo Singapore

This book is a work of fiction. Names, characters, places, and incidents are products of the author's imagination or are used fictitiously. Any resemblance to actual events or locales or persons, living or dead, is entirely coincidental.

A MINSTREL PAPERBACK *Original*

A Minstrel Book published by
POCKET BOOKS, a division of Simon & Schuster Inc.
1230 Avenue of the Americas, New York, NY 10020

ISBN: 0-671-52051-2

First Minstrel Books printing June 1995

10 9 8 7 6 5 4 3 2 1

Cover art by Aleta Jenks

Printed in the U.S.A.

To Michelle Gniazdowski

CHAPTER 1

I don't doodle in class. Not usually. But on this sunny March afternoon, I couldn't help it. I wrote my name and the name of our school team together on a piece of notebook paper.

```
                        L
                P A T T I
                A       O
                X       N
                T       S
R I C H A R D S O N
                N
```

At the front of the room Mr. Noonan was discussing the word *revolution.* Except he was the only one discussing. Nobody seemed to be really listening.

Mr. Noonan teaches seventh-grade history. But my mind wasn't on history. It was on cheering. I had on my cheerleading uniform—a blue skirt and a white sweater with a big yellow *P* on the front for Paxton. I had a basketball game to cheer for right after school!

I'd just started turning the *O*'s into little basketballs when Mr. Noonan said, "I have a surprise for you, class."

"Ooh! What, Mr. Noonan? What?" called Zena Lowey, waving her hand in the air. Zena's the big history class talker. She raises her hand for everything.

"We," said Mr. Noonan, "are about to begin a study of a fascinating time in history—the Russian Revolution!"

Suddenly another hand went up. When Mr. Noonan saw whose hand it was, he looked surprised. "Yes, Vanessa?" he said.

Vanessa Ivanova always sat in the back of the history room. The whole year I don't think she'd raised her hand once for class discussion. She always seemed off in a world of her own.

"I just wanted to say," began Vanessa in her breathy voice, "that my great-grandmother barely escaped Russia with her life. The Bolsheviks tried to murder her."

I stopped doodling. Suddenly history was getting interesting!

"Ah-ha!" exclaimed Mr. Noonan. He was nodding his head up and down. Maybe history was getting interesting for him, too.

"The Bolsheviks," he explained to the rest of us, "were workers and peasants who wanted to take over the Russian government from the Tsar.

"Vanessa," Mr. Noonan went on, "was your great-grandmother connected to the Romanovs, the royal family of Russia?"

"Yes," said Vanessa. "My mother says we should never forget that we have royal blood in our veins."

Wow! I thought. Sitting right here in a Paxton Junior High School history class was a real live Russian princess! The whole year I'd never talked to Vanessa. But I'd noticed her. Who wouldn't? She was one of the prettiest girls in seventh grade.

Vanessa was about my height—five-feet-one. But other than that, we were different. Like my mom, I'm blond and blue-eyed. Vanessa had long, dark, wavy hair and big, dark eyes. Like my mom, I wear my hair in a single braid going down my back. Vanessa wore hers loose. On rainy days it frizzed up in little curls all around her face. I didn't know exactly what I weighed. But it was about average for five-one. Vanessa was thin. Super thin.

I usually wore Gap shirts, jeans, and sneakers to school. Some girls wore T-shirts, leggings, and Doc Martens. Just about the only one who didn't stick to this unofficial PJHS dress code was my friend, Tara Miller. Tara wore weird miniskirts left over from the sixties. And a black leather jacket with fringe on the sleeves. Her taste was so weird!

Vanessa's clothes were different, too. But they were elegant. She wore silky tops and long chiffon skirts in dark colors—deep purples, rich browns, and blacks. When she walked into history class that first day, I thought she looked like an exotic butterfly coming into a room full of plain old moths.

"Do you know the story of your great-grandmother's escape from Russia?" Mr. Noonan was asking her.

"Yes," said Vanessa. "My great-grandmother, Natalia, and her husband, Peter, and their five children lived in St. Petersburg." Vanessa spoke dramatically. She sounded as if she were telling a story she'd heard many times before.

"That used to be the Russian capital," added Mr. Noonan.

"After the Revolution, they were all arrested. Even the children. With only the clothes on their backs, they were taken to jail. My great-grandmother and her little girls wore white muslin dresses with cloth-covered buttons."

I could tell Vanessa was repeating her story. The way she told it, it had the feel of a fairy tale.

"A few weeks later," she went on, "all the families in the jail were put on a train. The train took them to a small town in the mountains. For a year they lived there, growing their food in a small garden.

"Then one snowy day soldiers came with peasant carts," Vanessa continued. "As they forced everyone into the carts, Natalia became separated from her family. The carts went off in different directions. Natalia's cart was driven out of town to an abandoned mine shaft. It was very deep. The soldiers made the prisoners get out of the carts. They shoved them down into the mine. Then they threw huge rocks and logs on top of them!"

Several of us gasped.

"The soldiers threw hand grenades into the mine.

There was a huge explosion, and everyone was left for dead."

I couldn't believe my ears! I forgot about the basketball game. And about cheerleading. I forgot everything except Natalia.

"But Natalia survived," said Vanessa. "So did three others. To keep alive in the freezing cold, they took the clothes of those who did not survive. They put them on over their own clothes. Then they managed to climb out of the mine shaft. Natalia was frantic because she did not know what had become of her husband or her children. She wanted to look for them. But the other survivors were afraid she would be caught and give them away. So they forced her to come with them. At first they ran through the forest to get far away from the mine. Then they walked for weeks over the frozen tundra. By sneaking onto wagons and trains, they made their way west. In the spring, they caught a boat and escaped to Finland. Natalia still had . . ."

The three-fifteen bell rang. I jumped! It took me a minute to remember where I was—sitting at my desk in history.

"To be continued!" exclaimed Mr. Noonan. He was beaming at Vanessa. "This is just the kind of story that puts meat on the bones of history! Class, please read chapter six for Monday."

Gathering my papers, I thought of the only one of my great-grandmothers I knew about. Granny Nelly. Her full name was Nelly Keller—pretty plain. She was a teacher in a one-room schoolhouse in Texas. She wore checked gingham dresses. I knew, because I had a quilt she'd made from her old apron and dress scraps.

Why didn't my great-grandmother have a beautiful name like Natalia? Why wasn't she a cousin of the Tsar? How I wished that she had fled across the frozen tundra wearing a white muslin dress with cloth-covered buttons!

I walked down the hallway. Ahead of me, I saw Vanessa. Her black chiffon skirt swayed gently as she moved.

For the first time in my life, my cheerleading uniform didn't seem like the greatest outfit in the world. Suddenly it made me feel big and clunky. Especially the thick scrunch socks.

That's when I realized I was sick of being plain old Patti Richardson. Right then I would have given anything to be dressed in a gauzy, floaty black skirt. Just like Vanessa.

CHAPTER 2

Patti?" someone called. "Earth to Patti Richardson!"

I was walking toward the girls' locker room. I was still half in a daze, thinking about Vanessa's story.

I glanced behind me. "Oh, Tara," I said. "Hi!"

Tara's the alternate for the PJHS squad. Today she was cheering in place of an eighth-grader who had the flu. So she was wearing her cheerleading uniform, and not one of her crazy outfits.

"What's on your *head?*" I asked as she caught up with me.

"These?" she said, patting the front of her dark hair, where I saw six little plastic barrettes with pastel bunnies and baby chicks. "I'm letting my bangs grow out."

"My little sister's only seven," I told her, "and she won't even wear barrettes like that. She says they're babyish."

Tara rolled her eyes. "Baby barrettes are hip," she told me.

I opened the door to the girls' locker room. The place was buzzing with excitement. And no wonder!

The PJHS girls' basketball team was about to play Clayton. I was sure we'd win. In fact, everybody thought our girls' team was headed for the state championships! And if they went to state, some of the cheerleaders would get to go, too!

Okay, maybe I was getting psyched a little early. The team still had three games left to play in the season. But they'd already won nine games. They were first in our division. Undefeated! I just knew they'd go all the way to the top.

Getting excited over sports comes naturally to me, I guess. My dad played football for the University of Texas. Then he was a quarterback for the Dallas Cowboys. Now he sells copy machines. And he's the biggest football fan alive.

Everyone calls my mom Sunny. She and her twin sister, Peggy, were head cheerleaders at the University of Texas. Mom started me and my little sister, Missy, cheering early—at the age of four! Mom teaches aerobics classes now. But she says she still does a lot of cheerleading—getting those ladies to *move!*

Sometimes Tara talks like Dracula. "Pah-ti, dahlink!" she says. "Cheerleadink ees een your *blood!*" She's got that right!

Cheerleading sure was a lifesaver last August. That's when my family moved to Paxton. I'd lived in Dallas my whole life. I did *not* want to move to a place where I didn't know one single person. So I focused on trying out for cheerleading. I've never been happier than the day I became a Paxton cheerleader!

Now Tara and I made our way down the rows of lockers.

"I have that winning feeling," Susan Delgado, our squad captain, was saying. She has tan skin and silky black hair.

"Me, too!" called Deesha Taylor. Deesha's another seventh grader. She's dark complected and really strong because she's into weight training. "Nobody can go up against the Tower!"

"The Tower" was Liza Sears, the tallest girl on Paxton's basketball team. Tara had given her the nickname. It was a good one, too. The Sears Tower is the tallest building in Chicago, and Chicago's the closest big city to Paxton. Liza was just short of six feet. When she headed down the court with the ball, look out!

Tara and I walked down to the last row of lockers.

"Is my ponytail off center?" Cassie Copeland was asking Lauren Armstrong. Their lockers were directly across from Tara's and mine. Cassie whipped around, barely missing my face with the ends of her thick red hair.

"I can't tell," Lauren said. "You have too much hair!"

With her back to the long wall mirror, Cassie looked into a small hand mirror. She examined her ponytail. "It's crooked," she muttered, pulling out the elastic and starting over.

"I'm glad I'm not a hair perfectionist," Lauren declared.

Lauren had thick bangs. For cheering, she braided her hair in cornrows or wore a ponytail. It never looked sloppy. Maybe she'd figured out how to keep her hair neat when she was a gymnast. Lauren won two national gymnastics titles last year when she was twelve! Then she switched to cheerleading. Nobody can believe how many back flips she can do on our tumbling passes!

Tara, Cassie, and Lauren are my best friends on the squad. Back in August we were assigned to the same practice group at a cheerleading clinic. Ever since then, we've stuck together.

"Come on, Laur!" Tara was saying. "Just let me see what you'd look like without bangs. Please?" She began pinning Lauren's bangs back with baby barrettes.

"You look good without bangs, Lauren," Cassie said. "You have a high forehead. That's a sign of high intelligence." Cassie lifted up her own bangs then, to show her own high forehead.

I sat down on the bench and opened my locker.

"Do any of you guys know Vanessa Ivanova?" I asked.

"Sort of," said Cassie. She inspected her new ponytail in the mirror. "She takes ballet where I used to take. She's in the advanced level. But I saw her dance once when I took Madame Federova's open class on Saturday. She's *super* talented."

"You know what she told us in history?" I said.

"That her great-grandmother was a cousin of the King of Russia."

"You mean the Tsar," Cassie corrected me. But she didn't seem that impressed.

"There, done!" Tara grinned. She stepped back from Lauren.

Lauren checked her new hairstyle in the mirror. "I look like my little sister!" she exclaimed.

Tara kicked her locker shut. "Vanessa's the one who wears those long chiffon skirts, right?"

"Right," I said. "You know her?"

"She's in my English class," said Tara. "I've never talked to her. I just admire her skirts from afar. Her boots, too."

"Oh, I know who you're talking about," Lauren said. "Vanessa has a disgusting coat with *fur* on the hood. Somebody should clue her in that animals have rights!"

"Hey, guys! Let's go!" Susan Delgado yelled from the other side of the locker room. "Clayton's here!"

We all ran out of the locker room and into the gym.

"Check the bleachers," Tara said. "They're packed!"

Our players were dribbling and shooting baskets on the near side of the court. On the far side, Clayton was warming up.

Beth Ann Sorel, our cheerleading coach, called us together. Little blond Michelle Bostick began passing out our pom-poms.

We'd elected Michelle seventh-grade co-captain of the squad. Cassie ran against her and was so desperate to win that she tried to buy votes by giving presents! Naturally, that backfired and Michelle won. Cassie was so upset that she threatened to quit the squad. But Tara, Lauren, and I told her that if she quit, we'd quit, too. In the end nobody quit being a Paxton cheerleader.

"Let's cheer this team to another victory!" said Beth Ann.

"Let's do it! All right!" we all yelled. Deesha Taylor started circling her right arm over her head. This was a Texas cheerleading trick that I'd brought to Paxton. We all started circling our arms and yelling, *"Yaaaahooo!"* We were pumped!

The gym grew quiet. Liza and a girl from Clayton stood in center court, crouched down, face to face. The referee tossed the basketball up between them. Liza reached up and tapped it to Jade Moyer. Her feet never left the ground!

When Paxton was leading 18 to 4, Clayton called for a time out. Quickly we lined up, facing the stands. I stood by Cassie.

As we straightened our line, I caught sight of my mom and Missy in the bleachers. They were hard to miss! On top of her blond curls, Missy wore a bright blue baseball cap with a big yellow *P* on the front. Mom was waving a Paxton pennant.

Susan called, "Ready, *and!*"

Shoot for a basket!
Lions want to win!

All of us who were "bases"—the bottom girls in the stunts—jumped forward with our feet spread apart.

The "flyers"—the top girls—lined up behind us. I bent over, placing my hands on my knees. Cassie put her hands on my shoulders. Holding on, she popped up to stand on my thighs. She squeezed her knees together against me to keep her steady. Then she swung her arms out to the side. I reached up and got a firm grip under Cassie's arms.

B - A - S - K - E - T

Still gripping Cassie under the arms, I straightened up. Cassie kicked her legs out to the sides. Boom! She was sitting on my shoulders.

Put it in!

The crowd went wild! Cassie and the other flyers popped down. Lauren ended the cheer with a line of back handsprings.

As we ran back to the corner of the court, Beth Ann said, "Cassie, you looked light as a feather." She turned to me. "And Patti, you looked solid out there. Super sturdy."

I knew Beth Ann meant *solid* and *sturdy* as compliments. But for some reason the words made me feel big and clunky and heavy.

"Nachos!" announced my mom at our house later that night. She was carrying a big platter of the gooey cheese-and-chili-covered chips.

"Nachos!" cried Petey, our little green parakeet. *"Nachos!"*

Tara, Lauren, and Cassie were sleeping over. It was our Friday night tradition. Whenever the sleepover was at my house, we slept in the cartwheel room—a huge room with a wooden floor and big mirrors on two walls. Windows go all around above the mirrors. And there are skylights. The people who lived in our house before us built it as a dance studio for their daughters. Missy called it "the cartwheel room," and the name just stuck.

When we moved in, we filled the cartwheel room with lots of plants and with big, oversize pillows. We hung Petey's cage in the corner where the two mirrors meet.

"Yum!" Tara said, scooping up a big chip. "Thanks, Mrs. R."

"Yum," said Missy as she took one, too. "Thanks, Mom R."

Whenever Tara came over, Missy stuck to her like a tick to a dog. She tried to do everything Tara did. She even tried to dress like her! And Tara loved that Missy wanted to be just like her.

"This half's just cheese, no chili," Mom pointed out to Cassie and Lauren. Neither of them eats meat. "You girls know where the refrigerator is if you want anything else."

"Thanks, Mrs. Richardson," said Lauren.

"Missy," Mom said on her way out, "a few more minutes with the big girls. Then you run upstairs and I'll tuck you in."

"Okay, Mommy," Missy said agreeably. I could tell that she planned to stretch "a few minutes" into a *long* time.

"Seventy-four to thirty-six! What a win!" exclaimed Lauren as the four of us plus Missy sat down around the nachos.

"Liza is truly amazing!" said Tara. She turned the platter so she could reach the chili nachos. "You'd better take some, Patti," she advised, "before I totally pig out."

"Go ahead," I told her. "I'm not having any."

"How come?" Lauren asked me.

"I feel like I need to lose a couple pounds," I said.

Lauren rolled her eyes. But she didn't really disagree.

"Ten consecutive wins," Cassie said, flipping through the pages of her little black notebook. Cassie keeps track of everything in there. "We'll be ready for Webster in two weeks."

Cassie, Lauren, and Tara kept talking about the game. But I lay back on my pillow. I looked out at the starless sky.

My thoughts drifted back to Vanessa. In my whole life I'd never met anybody like her. She didn't worry about the things that worried the rest of us—wearing the "in" clothes, talking to boys, or hiding our pimples. She was above all that. She seemed perfectly happy in her own private world. I just knew that Vanessa had some secrets. Secrets that the rest of us might never learn. She was mysterious and beautiful and thin and elegant and graceful—everything that I longed to be.

"There's a star," Cassie said.

"First star," said Tara. "Make a wish, Missy."

" 'Star light, star bright,' " my little sister chanted.

She finished the poem, scrunched her eyes shut, and wished.

Looking up at that star, I made a wish of my own: *I wish I could be good friends with Vanessa.*

CHAPTER 3

In a way Mr. Noonan helped my wish come true.

"Vanessa?" he said on Monday afternoon. "We'd gotten your great-grandmother Natalia on a boat to Finland."

Vanessa smiled. "While she was living in St. Petersburg, my great-grandmother had prepared her family for an emergency. She took apart her diamond necklace and sewed the diamonds inside the cloth-covered buttons of her white dress. She sewed smaller diamonds inside the buttons of her daughter's dresses.

"In Finland Natalia sold her diamonds, one by one. This gave her money to live on. She spent her life writing letters to people who might know what had become of Peter and her children. Years later she discovered that they had survived. But Natalia never saw them again."

"That's so sad!" cried Emily Greer, who sat in front of me.

Zena's hand shot into the air. "I have a question!"

"I'm afraid you'll have to save it, Zena," said Mr. Noonan. "We have a lot of material to cover today."

Mr. Noonan took over then. History became less interesting. Near the end of class he said, "For the rest of our study of revolutionary Russia, I'd like you to pick a partner. You're going to do a report on an important person in Russian history."

"A written report?" asked Zena.

"An oral report," said Mr. Noonan. "Your reports are due the week of April seventh. That gives you three weeks to prepare."

As Mr. Noonan talked, Emily turned in her desk. She waggled her eyebrows at me. I thought she meant, "Let's be partners."

Mr. Noonan said we'd have class time to work. But we'd also need to work together outside of class. Then he pointed to a list on the board called Possible Subjects.

"A big part of this project is teamwork," Mr. Noonan said. "You and your research partner will receive just *one* grade for this report. It will be fifty-percent of this quarter's grade."

"Fifty percent!" gasped Zena. "That's so much!"

Mr. Noonan just nodded. "Now, choose a partner and discuss which person you'd like to study. When you've decided, come up and tell me. Subjects are first-come, first-serve."

I hoped Emily would forgive me. When Mr. Noonan gave the word, I sprang out of my desk. Before she had a chance to turn around again, I sprinted to the back of the room.

"Want to be partners?" I said as I reached Vanessa's desk.

At first Vanessa only stared at me with her big brown eyes.

"I thought about your story all weekend," I managed to say.

Now she looked pleased. "You did? About what part?"

"About your great-grandmother in her white dress with cloth-covered buttons," I said. I slid into the empty desk next to hers. "What happened to her husband and children anyway?"

Vanessa began another story then. She told me that Peter and the children were taken through the woods. Peter and some of the other men fought with the soldiers. They managed to take their guns. Then they escaped.

"They traveled south, where food was more plentiful," said Vanessa. "Several years later they returned to St. Petersburg."

"Wow," I said. Suddenly I remembered why I'd run back to Vanessa's desk. "Um, so, do you want to work together?" I asked.

Vanessa nodded. "Let's do our report on the Tsar."

"Great," I said. "I'll go tell Mr. Noonan."

Listening to Vanessa's story had taken some time. I ended up last in line. Emily Greer was first.

"Zena Lowey's my partner," Emily told Mr. Noonan.

I could tell Emily was thrilled about being partners with Zena. It guaranteed her an A plus on half of her report. I was glad. It meant she wouldn't be mad at me.

"We'd like to do our report on Rasputin," Emily said.

"He's sometimes called the mad monk," Mr. Noonan told her. He wrote down their choice. "Next!"

My turn finally came. I told Mr. Noonan that Vanessa and I were partners. "We'd like to do our report on the Tsar," I said.

"Tsar Nicholas is taken," Mr. Noonan said. "These subjects are left." Mr. Noonan pointed on the board to *Nicholas Nicolaievich* and *Felix Yussoupov.*

I'd never heard of them. I'd never be able to pronounce their names in an oral report! I didn't know what to do.

"Or King George of England," Mr. Noonan added. "He was the Tsar's cousin. No one's taken him yet."

"We'll take him," I said quickly. I wasn't sure what he had to do with Russia. But at least I could say his name!

"Fine," said Mr. Noonan, writing it down. "I'll expect an excellent report from you two," he said. "Something that will put plenty of meat on the bones of history!"

I walked back to Vanessa. "The Tsar was already taken," I told her. "We got his cousin, King George of England."

Vanessa wrinkled her nose. "Yuck!" she said. "Who cares about him?"

The next day our history class went to the library. Vanessa and I sat at a small table tucked behind the magazine shelf.

Vanessa had on a silky brown blouse with scallops around the neck and a long brown chiffon skirt. She had on brown tights and the brown lace-up boots that Tara liked. I'd always thought brown was a dull color. But on Vanessa, it looked elegant.

I had on jeans and a plain blue top. It had a little ivory ribbon threaded through loops around the neck. It used to be my favorite shirt. But now it felt pretty ordinary.

"I'll check the Subject Guide," I volunteered.

But everybody was already crowded around the Guide. I came back to our table. "It's mobbed," I told Vanessa. "I'll have to try again in a few minutes."

"Okay," said Vanessa. She started drawing a toe shoe on the top of her paper.

"Oh, Cassie Copeland's a good friend of mine," I told her. "She used to take ballet at Madame Federova's. Do you know her?"

Vanessa shook her head "no." She began attaching spirals of ribbon to the shoes.

"Cassie said you were in a higher class," I added quickly.

"I'm in Level Six," she said. "It's the advanced class. Most of the other girls are sixteen. I take class on Monday, Tuesday, Thursday, Friday, and Saturday." She sighed. "If the school were open on Wednesday and Sunday, I'd take class then, too."

"Wow. Cassie said you were really good."

"I have good feet and good turnout," Vanessa said. "I inherited them from my grandmother, Tamara."

"Tamara?" I repeated the beautiful name.

"Natalia's daughter," Vanessa said. "She was a ballerina."

"She was?" Vanessa had *another* fascinating ancestor! "Where did she dance? In Russia?"

Vanessa nodded. "After the bad times Peter and the children returned to St. Petersburg."

As Vanessa began telling the story, her voice changed. I knew she was telling it just the way it had been told to her. It cast a spell over me.

"Tamara and Ivan, one of her brothers, began attending ballet school. At this time the school had no money. In the winter there was no heat. The poor ballerinas had to wear long underwear beneath their costumes. Still, many dancers came down with pneumonia and died."

"That's terrible!"

"Tamara was lucky," Vanessa went on. "She didn't get sick. She danced for hours every day. At twenty she was the star of the ballet. Everyone wanted to see Tamara Volinsky dance. Then one day the company received an invitation to dance in Paris."

Vanessa leaned closer to me. "Many dancers planned to go and never return to Russia. Conditions there were too bad."

"Did Tamara go?" I asked.

"Yes," said Vanessa. "But a group of soldiers came to the train station. Their leader demanded to see Tamara's papers. He discovered that she had only a one-way ticket."

"What did he do?"

"He said, 'You may go to Paris, Tamara Volinsky.

But you will never dance there.' She was very bold. She said, 'How will you stop me?' And do you know what he did?"

I shook my head.

"He pulled a long curved sword from a scabbard that hung on his belt. And he brought it down across the back of her ankle."

I was speechless!

"My grandmother Tamara had studied ballet from the age of nine," Vanessa said. "She had taken class with icicles hanging from the heating pipes. She had perfected her art. Then, with one swift stroke of a sword, that soldier ended everything. He sliced through her tendon." Vanessa looked down in her lap. "Tamara never danced again. She never walked again without a cane."

"That's the worst thing I've ever heard," I breathed.

We weren't exactly getting organized for our report. But I sure was learning a lot of Russian history!

"I take five classes a week now," Vanessa went on. "Sometimes six, if I take two classes on Saturday."

"That's so many!" I exclaimed.

"But not enough," Vanessa said. "Some day I'll study at the School of American Ballet in New York City. I'll take two or three classes a day!" She looked happy, just thinking of that. "I'll finish my training there. Then I'll join a ballet company."

Wow, I thought. Vanessa knows what she wants to do when she grows up. I didn't even know what I wanted to do next weekend!

I glanced up. Emily and Zena were still pouring over the Subject Guide.

"We might as well look at some magazines," Vanessa whispered. She tiptoed over to the shelf and picked out two teen magazines. She brought them to our table. Together, we leafed through page after page of models wearing new spring fashions.

"Do you like that outfit?" I asked, pointing to a girl in a blue halter top and shorts.

"Yuck!" said Vanessa. "She's too fat to be wearing that!"

"You think she's *fat?"* I said. She didn't look fat to me.

Vanessa nodded. "Look at her thighs. Even the tops of her arms are fat. She's gross!" Quickly she turned the page. "Now *she* is just right." Vanessa smoothed the page with her hand.

To me, that model looked super skinny.

"You're so thin," I said. "How do you do it? I've hardly eaten anything for three days. But I don't feel any thinner."

"I'll show you," Vanessa said. She opened the zippered compartment in her notebook. She pulled out a small book called *Fat-free Eating.* I'd seen little books like it at supermarket checkout counters. She also took out a tiny notebook. A pen was stuck through the spiral of wire at the top.

"This tells how many grams of fat are in different foods," she said, pointing to *Fat-free Eating.* "You can borrow it."

"Okay," I said. "Thanks!"

"I've been keeping track of fat for so long I've got the whole book memorized anyway." She opened the little notebook. "This is my Fat Book," she explained. "I write down everything I eat. I stay under nine hundred calories a day. And no more than six grams of fat. See?"

I examined her notebook. Then I looked back at *Fat-free Eating.* "Wow, one pat of butter has four grams of fat! Six grams a day isn't very many, is it?"

"I never touch butter." Vanessa pretended to shudder. "If you want, I'll help you make a Fat Book."

"Oh, great!" I said. "I'd love that."

"Get a really teensy notebook," she advised. "So you can keep it with you all the time. Call me tonight. I'll tell you how to set it up. Here's my number." She wrote it on one of the pages of her Fat Book, tore it out, and handed it to me. "I have my own number," she said. "It's unlisted. So don't lose this."

"Don't worry," I told her. "I won't."

I'd just learned *two* of Vanessa's secrets! Her Fat Book. And her secret phone number! My wish was starting to come true. I was getting to be good friends with Vanessa.

CHAPTER 4

Wednesday, March 19

Breakfast:

Cereal	Calories: 240	Fat: 2 gr.
Blueberries	Calories: 40	Fat: 0 gr.
Milk	Calories: 100	Fat: 2 gr.
Orange Juice	Calories: 110	Fat: 0 gr.
Total:	Calories: 490	Fat: 4 gr.

I'd asked Mom for one of the small notebooks she uses for her shopping lists. In it, I'd started my very own Fat Book. Boy, was I surprised! I'd eaten what I thought was a little bitty breakfast. But it had *lots* of calories.

Tucking my Fat Book inside my notebook, I ran downstairs. Mom drove me to school. I went straight to the library. Mr. Noonan had ordered special research books from the Paxton Public Library. Mr. Marten, the librarian, helped me find three of them: *The Letters of Nicholas and George, The Last Days of the Tsar,* and *A King's Story.* My heart sank when I saw them. They were all big, thick books with teeny-tiny print.

"Yuck!" exclaimed Vanessa when she walked into history class that afternoon. "What are those?"

"Books on King George," I said glumly. "For our report. We didn't get too much done yesterday, so I got these." I shrugged. "Anyway, want to see a picture of King George and the Tsar?"

"Not really," she said, kneading a spot on her calf. "We did a new variation at ballet yesterday. I think I pulled a muscle."

I knew what that felt like. Cheering was pretty hard on muscles, too.

"Ever try Icy Hot?" I asked.

Vanessa brightened. "All the time," she said. "I hate the way it smells. But it really works. How come you use it?"

"Cheerleading," I said. But I didn't really want to talk about cheerleading with Vanessa. "I took ballet for a while," I added. "In Texas—when I was little."

"Really?" said Vanessa. "Were you good?"

"Not very," I said. "When we did the 'reach for the cherries' part, I could never reach very high."

"When you did *what?*" Vanessa squealed.

Mr. Noonan and several kids looked over at us.

Vanessa put a hand over her mouth. Quickly we both looked down, as if studying the King George books. But really we were trying not to burst out laughing.

"When you did *what?"* Vanessa whispered, still giggling.

"Our teacher, Miss Ashley, had us pretend to be picking cherries," I whispered back.

Vanessa rolled her eyes. "Go on."

"She had us reach way up to a high branch." I could almost hear Miss Ashley's voice saying, *"Stretch up and pluck a cherry!"*

Vanessa kept her hand pressed firmly over her mouth.

"Then, keeping our legs straight," I went on, "we bent down and put the cherry in the bucket."

Vanessa gave a little squeal of laughter. She swiftly propped *A King's Story* up in front of her face so Mr. Noonan wouldn't see. Her whole body shook with the giggles.

By now my face was beet red.

"Come on!" I said, giggling, too. "I was only about eight!"

Vanessa just shook her head. "What music did you dance to?"

"I can't remember," I said. "Miss Ashley played different tapes." No way was I going to admit that my favorite song had been "Pop Goes the Weasel"!

Vanessa caught her breath. "That is so funny!" she said. "You should try taking a *real* ballet class some time."

"Maybe," I said. "I could practice at home. We have a ballet studio in our house."

"You have *what?*" Vanessa said in a hushed tone. Her eyes were wide. She wasn't giggling anymore.

I explained why it was there. "It's got a great floor for jumping," I went on. "My sister calls it the cart-wheel room."

"Patti," Vanessa said, "can I come over and see it?" She grabbed my arm. "Maybe try dancing in it?"

"Sure," I said. I was so happy that she wanted to come over!

"How about today?" she said. "After school?"

"Well, not today. I have cheerleading practice."

Vanessa pressed her lips together, thinking. At last her eyes lit up. "I know!" she whispered. "Saturday! Madame gives an open class at ten. Anyone can take it. Why don't you come?"

"Oh, I don't think so," I said. "I mean, I wasn't even very good at cherry-picking ballet!"

"Who would be? Come on!" she coaxed. "Madame's husband plays lots of Mozart. You'll love it! And then we'll go over to your house!"

"Are there any total beginners?" I asked.

"Lots!" promised Vanessa. "I take it to warm up for my Level Six class at eleven. It's great exercise. Doing a barre is the *best* way to trim down your thighs."

"Well, I could use a little of that," I said.

"Who couldn't?" said Vanessa. "So, you're coming, right?"

"Okay." I smiled over at Vanessa. "I'll come."

Suddenly Vanessa's smile faded. "It won't work. You'd have to wait around the studio until my eleven o'clock class is over."

"That's okay," I said.

"Really?" Vanessa's face lit up again.

"Oh, but wait. On Saturday I always meet my friends at the mall. Cassie Copeland, Tara Miller, and Lauren Armstrong. You know them, right?"

Vanessa shook her head.

"Anyway, we have lunch. Then we shop and stuff. Hey, I know! Why don't you come, too?"

Vanessa rolled her eyes. *"Then* we'll go to your house?"

"Sure," I said. "See if you can stay for dinner, okay? Then when Tara and everybody go home, we can work on our report."

"Sounds perfect!" Vanessa smiled.

I was sure Cassie, Lauren, and Tara would like Vanessa. We'd all hang out in the cartwheel room. We'd listen to music and talk. Maybe Vanessa would tell more of her stories.

"About the ballet class," Vanessa said. "You can wear any color leotard. Do you have ballet shoes? If you don't, I can lend you a pair. I have zillions."

I glanced down at Vanessa's pretty lace-up boots. They looked like about a size three!

"No, that's okay," I said quickly. No way was I going to tell her I wore a size seven! "I can get a pair."

"Well, how about ti—" Vanessa stopped.

Mr. Noonan was standing over our desks. He was just looking down at us. How long had he been there? I wondered.

"I never knew King George's life was so amusing," he said.

"I'm sorry, Mr. Noonan," I murmured.

I glanced at Vanessa. She looked as if she were about to burst out laughing. Worried, I glanced back at Mr. Noonan. But he didn't look mad. In fact, he smiled at Vanessa!

"Get to work, girls," was all he said.

That night after I picked at my dinner I went upstairs to my new room. We'd lived in Paxton for eight months now. But I still thought of my bedroom as my *new* room. Just before we moved in, Mom had it papered with blue-and-white striped wallpaper. My bed, dresser, dressing table, and even my desk are all white wicker. Folded on the foot of my bed was Granny Nelly's faded old quilt.

"Hey, Patti?" Missy bounded into my room. "It's 'Lucy Month'!"

"It's what?" I asked. I opened the top drawer of my dresser. I dug around for a pair of tights.

"There are two 'I Love Lucy,' shows on every night for a month," Missy explained.

"Yeah?" I was a major Lucy fan. Everybody in my family was.

"Want to watch it, Patti?" asked Missy. "Mom and Dad are."

"I don't think so," I said. I began rummaging in the middle drawer. "I have things to do."

"Okay," said Missy as she skipped out the door. "But I hope you change your mind."

Finally I found an old pink leotard I'd worn in a

gymnastics class. I found a pair of white tights from last Easter. They'd do. I got dressed. Then I opened my closet door, where there was a full-length mirror. I took a good look.

I wasn't fat. But as Beth Ann had said, I was sturdy and solid. The more I looked at my legs, the more sturdy and solid they seemed. Like tree trunks.

I ran down the hall to Mom and Dad's bathroom. I hopped on their scale. The needle pointed to 105. I couldn't remember what I'd weighed last time I went for a checkup. But I thought it was less than that.

Well, it was only Wednesday. Back in my room I opened my Fat Book. I'd written down everything I'd had to eat all day. Even though I'd just eaten an apple and one slice of bread for lunch, I'd managed to eat almost 1,200 calories! That was too many. I'd do better tomorrow. By Saturday I'd weigh less.

Downstairs, I walked through the living room. On TV I saw Lucy dressed up like Harpo Marx. I loved that episode! When the real Harpo shows up, Lucy tries to make him think he's looking into a mirror by doing *exactly* what he does.

"Hey, Patti-cakes," Dad said. He muted the TV's sound as a commercial came on. "What are you up to?"

My dad has short brown hair. His nose is bumpy and a little bit crooked. That's because he kept breaking it when he played football. He always says *"Better my nose than my throwing arm."* Now he was snuggled up on the couch next to Mom. He had his throwing arm around her shoulder.

"I'm going to practice dancing, Daddy," I told him.

"Mom?" I whispered as Dad clicked the sound back on. "Have we got any tapes of classical music?"

"I don't know, sugar," Mom whispered back. "You'll have to look."

What we had were country-and-western tapes. And hits from the sixties. Mom and Dad loved that old Righteous Brothers song, "Unchained Melody." Whenever it came on, they always rushed into each others arms and slow danced. As Vanessa would say, *Yuck!*

I turned on the radio. I fiddled with the dial until I found Cassie's father's station. They were playing something I thought was classical music. At least nobody was singing.

I went over to the barre. I tried to remember what I'd learned in Miss Ashley's class. First position. I bent my knees. And straightened. Second position. It was coming back to me.

I'd been at it for half an hour when Missy zoomed in.

"Tah-dah!" she cried. She held her arms out and twirled around. She was dressed in an old black leotard. "Will you show me your dance routine, Patti?"

"I'm just practicing ballet," I said.

"Like at Miss Ashley's?" said Missy.

"Sort of. But no picking cherries. This is *serious* ballet."

"I'll practice with you," Missy offered.

Every time I bent my knees, Missy bent down. Every time I leaned to the side, Missy leaned, too. Whatever I did, she did it, too. Sometimes I didn't mind having Missy around all that much. Tonight was one of those times.

CHAPTER 5

Thanks, Mrs. Miller!" I called as I got out of her car.

Our Friday night sleepover had been at Tara's apartment. Tara's mom had just dropped me off at home on her way to work on Saturday morning.

"You're welcome!" Mrs. Miller called back. "Have fun at ballet!"

At Tara's I'd gotten all ready for the class. I woke up at seven. I stretched and showered and rubbed half a stick of deodorant under my arms. I didn't want to stink! I wound my hair into a bun and stuck it to the back of my head with a dozen bobby pins. I put on my leotard and tights. Then I put on my T-shirt and jeans over them. I was ready. At least I hoped I was.

Inside our house I walked back to the kitchen. Mom and Dad were sitting at the table. Their heads were close together. They were giggling over something in the newspaper. Mom kissed Dad on the back of his neck and started to get up from her chair. But Dad grabbed her and pulled her into his lap.

"Whoa, Bill!" Mom whooped as he started kissing her neck.

I stomped over to the counter. I mean, did they have to do this stuff at nine o'clock in the morning?

"Patti!" Mom exclaimed when she saw me. "How about some melon, honey?" She stood up. "And some French toast?"

"Mom," I whispered when she came over to me, "can you guys not act like that when everybody comes over this afternoon?"

"Act like what?"

"You know. Don't kiss in front of my friends."

"Now, Patti . . ." Mom launched into her lecture on how lucky I was to have two parents who loved each other so much. At the end she added, "Okay, now, what can I fix you for breakfast?"

"I ate breakfast, Mom. At Tara's. I had juice and toast."

"Juice and toast are not enough to fuel your engine," Mom said. "You need protein, honey. Something to stick to your ribs."

"Really, Mom. I ate."

"Patrice Richardson"—Mom always uses our full names when she means business—"Have a bowl of cereal. I don't want you leaving this house without a good solid breakfast."

There was that word again: *solid!* It wasn't any use arguing with Mom when she got like this. But there was no way I could take a ballet class with cereal gurgling around in my stomach!

"I'll eat a granola bar on the way to the studio. Okay?"

Mom looked at her watch. "It'll have to be, won't it?" she said. "If you want to get there by nine-thirty, we'd better move."

A minute later I was sitting in the van next to Mom. She drove out of our subdivision through the big iron BERKSHIRE gate. I nibbled nervously on the granola bar. Five minutes later we pulled up in front of a white two-story wooden building off Main Street. A sign said FEDEROVA BALLET STUDIO.

"Let me make sure I've got the plans straight," Mom said. "At twelve-thirty you and Vanessa are walking to the mall to meet Tara, Cassie, and Lauren?"

"Right," I said. "And I've got the money you gave me for new school clothes."

"How about buying one of those nice blue denim shirts from the Gap? It sure would bring out the blue of your eyes!"

"Maybe," I said.

If Mom wasn't dressed in a warm-up suit, she wore blue denim. One of her big thrills in life was for her and Missy and me to dress alike. Maybe it's because she's a twin—I don't know. To tell the truth, I was getting tired of it.

"Well, just be sure everything you get is practical, Patti. Check the tags. Make sure they say *machine washable.*"

"Okay, Mom."

"I'll pick you all up at four. And bring everyone back to our house for a big supper."

"Thanks, Mom!" I slid out of the van. Slinging my bag over my shoulder, I ran up the steps and into a large lobby. Piano music tinkled from behind a door. On the floor lots of girls were stretching. I didn't see Vanessa. Stepping carefully around arms and legs, I walked to a desk on the far side of the room. A small, dark-haired woman sat behind it.

"Hi!" I said to her. Yikes! My voice sounded so loud. Except for the faint piano music, it was very quiet.

"I'd like to take the ten o'clock class," I whispered.

"Eight dollars, please," the woman said with a heavy accent.

I gave her my money. Then she tapped a finger on a book that lay open on the desk. It was filled with signatures. The first one under *10:00* was *Vanessa Ivanova.* I switched my granola bar to my other hand and signed my name at the bottom of the list.

"Dressing room," the woman said, pointing down the hallway.

"Oh, okay," I said, nodding. "Thank you!"

I walked down the narrow hallway to the dressing room. It was dimly lit. It had wooden cubbies with hooks rather than lockers. Socks, leg warmers, and ballet bags littered the floor.

A bony girl sitting on a bench looked up at me. "You know how many grams of fat that has?" she asked.

"What, this granola bar?" I said. "Um, not really."

"Ten!" she said. "Look at the label."

I looked. She was right! I'd have to be more careful!

As I tossed the rest of the bar into the trash, I saw Vanessa. She was talking to a girl in a white leotard. Her eyes flicked in my direction. But she just kept talking.

Vanessa's long wavy hair was pulled back into a bun. It made her head look small. I knew she was thin. But at school her long blouses and billowy skirts covered her up. Here, dressed in a dark green leotard and pink tights, she looked positively skinny!

I sat down on a bench and took off my street clothes. I put on my new black ballet slippers. I stuffed my clothes into my bag. For a minute I felt bad that Vanessa was ignoring me. But then I remembered how many years she'd taken ballet here. Of course she had lots of friends. Probably she was in the middle of a really important conversation with the white-leotard girl.

I sat on the bench, fiddling with things in my bag. This sure was different from getting dressed for cheerleading practice. There, everybody was real friendly. We all talked a mile a minute or yelled across the room. Here, the girls seemed to whisper. If they talked at all.

Outside the dressing room the music stopped. I heard faint applause. A few seconds later the dressing room door swung open. Hot, sweaty dancers began streaming in. Every one of them, I noticed, was wearing *pink* ballet slippers.

"Come on, Patti!" Vanessa said. Suddenly she was

standing right in front of me. "You have to get a good spot at the barre."

Slinging my bag over my shoulder, I hurried after her.

In the studio Vanessa threw her huge ballet bag into a pile at the side of the room. I did the same. Then Vanessa walked me over to the middle of a long barre.

"Stand here," she said. "I have to work at the center barre. Madame likes me to demonstrate."

"Okay," I whispered back.

Vanessa scurried over to the center barre.

Now an elderly woman with coal-black hair walked through the door. She looked like a slightly younger sister of the woman sitting behind the desk in the lobby.

"First position," she said, nodding to the pianist. He began to play. And it wasn't "Pop Goes the Weasel" either!

At first the barre exercises were easy. For one we reached a hand up over our heads and brought it slowly down to our feet. Catching Vanessa's eye, I mouthed *cherry picking!*

Vanessa looked away. Her expression never changed. Maybe she goofed around in history. But not in ballet class.

Soon the exercises became harder. When I didn't understand Madame's instruction, I watched Vanessa. I copied what she did.

After the barre we gathered in a corner of the studio. Madame asked us to get into groups of three. I got into a group with the girls I'd stood next to at the barre. Each group took turns leaping across to the opposite corner of the studio. My group was first. I tried to leap. But I couldn't seem to get off the ground.

Then it was Vanessa's group's turn. Vanessa looked like a professional dancer already. When she leaped, she did it so naturally. She just seemed to belong up in the air.

"She's amazing, isn't she?" a girl in my group whispered.

"I love to watch her jump," the other girl added.

Jump? Hey, maybe I couldn't leap. But I could *jump!* I'd been doing cheerleading jumps my whole life! I watched the next group. Their leaps were like my favorite cheerleading jumps—Herkies! When it was my group's turn again, I gave it my all. I sprang up. I did a perfect split in the air! My landing wasn't totally smooth. I had to take a few hops to catch my balance. But I jumped again. This time I came down a little bit better.

"Height, good," Madame said as I walked past her. "On landing, bend knees more."

After several more jumps I was feeling pretty good. Then Madame said, "That will be all."

We clapped. Then we walked over to pick up our bags.

Vanessa sat down and opened her ballet bag. She tossed out leotards, tights, a bathrobe, hair clips, and gum wrappers before she pulled out a pair of pink satin toe shoes.

"You're great, Vanessa!" I told her. "Really great!"

"Thanks," Vanessa said as she tied her toe shoe ribbons. "You're waiting for me, right?"

"Right," I said.

"Don't get bored and leave or anything."

"I wouldn't do that." How could she think I would?

Vanessa beamed me a smile. "Okay," she said. "I just can't wait to see that studio!"

I grinned. I couldn't wait to show it to her!

CHAPTER 6

I've seen you dance," Cassie said to Vanessa when we arrived at Yogurt Palace in the mall. "At Madame's. You're really good."

"Thanks," Vanessa said. She slid in across from me at the booth. After ballet she'd changed into a rose-colored shirt and long skirt. Instead of boots today, she had on black flats.

"I don't take ballet anymore," Cassie told her. "I switched to cheerleading."

"So, what's it going to be, guys?" Tara asked. "The usual?" She turned to Vanessa. "The usual's a Strawberry Mountain," she explained. "A humongous yogurt with six different toppings."

"I'll just have water," Vanessa said. "With lemon."

"That's *all* you're having?" Lauren exclaimed.

"I'm never hungry right after ballet class," Vanessa said.

"Yeah, I'm not hungry, either," I echoed.

"You're just having *water,* Patti?" asked Tara.

My eyes skimmed the menu. "I'll have an iced tea," I said.

"So that means just three of us are splitting the Mountain?" Tara sounded a little huffy.

"I can demolish a third," said Lauren.

"Me, too," said Cassie.

Tara and I went up to the counter to place our order. When we came back to the table, Cassie and Vanessa were talking excitedly.

"I saw the New York City Ballet in Chicago," Cassie said.

"Aren't they amazing?" said Vanessa. Her eyes were sparkling. "What ballets did you see?"

"*The Concert* was my favorite," Cassie said.

"Oh, I love that one!" exclaimed Vanessa. "It's *so* funny!"

"Funny?" Lauren said. "I've never seen a funny ballet."

"Yeah, me, either," I put in quickly. Of course, I'd never seen *any* ballet! I wished they'd change the subject.

I popped up to get our order. I carried everything to our booth on a tray. That Strawberry Mountain looked so *good!* It was covered with M&M's, candy corn, rainbow sprinkles, chocolate sprinkles, coconut shavings, and Reese's Pieces. It was all I could do to keep myself from digging in! But I didn't. I didn't want a Strawberry Mountain messing up my Fat Book!

"The man with the deep voice on 'Mozart in the Morning' on WBMG?" Lauren was saying to Vanessa. "That's Cassie's father!"

"Really?" Vanessa's eyebrows arched way up. "Wow! It must be so cool to have a father who's in show business!"

"Oh, it is," said Cassie. "It definitely is. Listen, Vanessa, you want me to get you a WBMG nightshirt? They gave them away during last year's pledge drive. One size fits all. They've got big pictures of Mozart on the front."

"Cool!" said Vanessa. "What color are they?"

"Lavender, powder blue, pink, black, or white."

"Hey, Cassie!" exclaimed Tara. "How come you've never asked us if we wanted nightshirts?"

Cassie shrugged. "I didn't think you were so big on Mozart."

"He's my favorite," I said. "And blue's my color."

"I'll take lavender," said Lauren.

"Black for me," said Tara. *"If* it's one hundred percent cotton."

"It is," said Cassie. "So, Vanessa?"

"Pink would be great," said Vanessa. "But I *love* white, too. I don't know which to pick! What do you think?"

"I'll bring you both," Cassie offered.

"Spaseebo!" said Vanessa.

"Wait a minute!" said Cassie. "I can answer that!" She was waving her hands around in the air. "I know! *Ne za shto.* That is Russian for 'you're welcome.' "

I glanced at Tara and Lauren. They looked puzzled, too.

Vanessa and Cassie sure were getting along. I'd

wanted them to! But all the talk about ballet and classical music and now Russian made me feel so out of it.

"Nash Kent's father taught me," Cassie was explaining. "He teaches Russian at Clayton High. Nash and I are sort of going out. You know him?"

Vanessa shook her head. It was hard to believe she didn't know Nash Kent! He'd led our basketball team to victory two years in a row. *Everybody* at PJHS knew him—except Vanessa.

Not much was left of the Strawberry Mountain now. But to me, even the soupy remains at the bottom of the dish looked tempting. I'd finished my iced tea. I'd chewed all the ice cubes. I'd eaten the sprig of mint. And the lemon wedge—rind and all! I was ready to gnaw the glass! Instead, I started biting my thumbnail.

Across from me Vanessa hadn't even finished her water.

Without noticing, I'd bitten off all my nails on my right hand. Oh, well. Who wanted one great-looking hand and one nibbled hand? I started in on my left thumbnail.

"Okay, guys," said Tara. "Let's hit the shops! But first, let's hit the bathroom."

"I'll go with you," said Cassie.

I followed Lauren and Vanessa out of Yogurt Palace. As I walked, I promised myself a few things. Next trip to the video store, I'd rent a ballet tape. And before school I'd listen to "Mozart in the Morning," too. Every morning! Next time we came to Yogurt Palace, I wouldn't be so out of it. By then I'd be a brand-new me.

I tuned into what Lauren was saying. "My little sister's taken over my jean jacket," she said to Vanessa. "It's huge on her, but she loves it. So my mom said I could get a new one."

"Hmmm," said Vanessa.

"Do you have a big family?" Lauren asked her.

"Just my parents and my grandfather, and me."

"Any pets?" asked Lauren.

Vanessa shook her head.

"I *love* animals," Lauren said. "Especially furry ones."

Uh-oh! I could tell Lauren was about to bring up Vanessa's fur-trimmed jacket! "Let's hit the Gap," I suggested quickly.

"Let's not," whined Tara as she and Cassie found us. "They never have any truly outrageous stuff."

Lauren grabbed Tara by the elbow. "This'll take ten minutes," she said, pulling her toward the Gap. "Come on."

At the Gap Tara and Lauren checked out the jean jackets. Cassie and I wandered from rack to rack. Vanessa did, too. But she didn't look at the clothes. She held on to the racks as if they were ballet barres. She twirled and pliéd and did little jumps.

"Patti?" Vanessa said as we reached a rack of blue denim shirts. "What time is your mom picking us up?"

"Four," I said.

"So late?" Vanessa made a funny face. "I can't wait to see that studio!"

"The cartwheel room?" asked Cassie. "You'll love it!"

"Do you like these denim shirts, Vanessa?" I asked.

"They're not bad," she said, slipping into fifth position.

"Yeah," I agreed. "Not bad. But not good, either."

"Your chiffon skirts are great, Vanessa," Cassie said.

"Thanks," said Vanessa. She pushed off from the rack and twirled on one foot. Her skirt flared out around her.

"Done!" Lauren exclaimed. She walked toward us holding a blue bag with white lettering. Tara was at her side.

"Okay, let's check out some boutique windows," Tara said. "Let's see if anything speaks to us!"

We walked up and down the hallways, looking in shop windows. About every other one had something that "spoke" to Tara. So we went in and tried on clothes. Cassie bought a black vest. Lauren bought a red, white, and blue ski sweater on sale. Tara tried on the craziest item in every store. I didn't see anything I liked.

Vanessa didn't try on anything. She just followed us around, turning and stretching and twirling. Half the time I didn't think she even knew what store we were in.

"Maybe you should call your mom, Patti," Vanessa whispered as we left Shell's Music, where I bought a Mozart tape. "Maybe she can pick us up early."

"Mom's teaching her aerobics class now, so she can't."

Vanessa squeezed her eyes shut. "Oh, I want to get there! I can't help it!" she said, doing impatient little jumps.

"Impressions is down this way," Tara said. "It has good sales."

We all stopped and gazed at the Impressions window display.

"Vanessa!" exclaimed Lauren. "This looks like you!"

Right away I saw what she meant. One mannequin was dressed in a long, maroon cotton sweater and a long maroon chiffon skirt.

"Is this where you get your skirts?" Cassie asked.

"No," Vanessa said.

"Well, where do you get them?" asked Cassie bluntly.

"I have a dressmaker," Vanessa said with a twirl.

A dressmaker! Now I knew another of Vanessa's secrets!

"You mean someone makes all your clothes?" asked Cassie.

"Just for me," said Vanessa. She twirled on one foot again.

I stared at the maroon outfit. What would it look like on me? Maybe, if I wore that, I'd look elegant.

"Um . . . Maybe I should try that on," I said. "What do you think, guys?"

"Hey, yeah!" said Tara. "This could be a whole new you!"

I glanced at Tara as the five of us walked into the store. How did she know I'd been thinking about a *new me?*

"Go into the dressing room, Patti," Tara said. "We'll be your personal shoppers and bring you different outfits."

I looked at the sales clerk. She gave a little nod. After all, we were the only customers in the store.

In the dressing room I sat down. I tried not to think about my growling stomach. Or how I felt a headache coming on. I'd been getting them a lot lately.

Half a minute later Tara brushed aside the curtain. "Tah-dah!" She held up a shiny sleeveless black dress.

"Not a chance," I said. "What's that made out of anyway?"

"Vinyl," said Tara. "When it gets dirty, you just sponge it off. Isn't that cool?"

"It's disgusting," I said. Tara looked disappointed.

Tara went away then and Vanessa appeared. "Here's a skirt and sweater like the ones in the window," she said.

"Thanks, Vanessa." I took the hangers from her and she left.

I pulled on the sweater. Perfect fit. The waist of the skirt was tight, though. *Really* tight. But that was okay. I was going to lose some weight. In a couple of weeks it would fit just fine.

I checked the price. I had enough money. But the outfit was all I could buy. I wouldn't be able to buy any school clothes.

I checked myself in the dressing room mirror. I didn't look like plain old Patti anymore! But I didn't look like Vanessa, either. I flashed on my little sister playing dress-up! The hem of the skirt almost touched the toes of my sneakers. Twirling, I felt the skirt billow out from my legs. Was this the *new me?*

"Are you coming out?" Lauren called.

Taking a deep breath, I stepped out of the dressing room and into the shop. In front of a three-way mirror I twirled again, just like Vanessa.

"So?" I said, looking from face to face.

For a moment no one spoke.

"It could work." Tara squinted at me. "But it's a *lot* of maroon. Maybe a belt would help. Or a scarf."

"Roll the skirt up at the waist," suggested Cassie.

"Just take it off!" said Lauren. "It is *not* you."

"No?" I said. I turned to Vanessa. "What do you think?"

"It looks great," Vanessa said as she pushed off on the mirror for another spin. "I think you should get it."

"Really?" I walked back and forth. I felt the silky fabric swish against my legs. I looked in the mirror again. Lauren was right. It wasn't me. But that was the whole point! I wanted to change. I wanted to be different from plain old Patti. So, I had to start somewhere. This outfit seemed the perfect way to begin.

I grinned at Vanessa. "Okay, I'm getting it," I said. After all, if Vanessa liked it on me, it *must* look great!

I got dressed then. I took the skirt and sweater up to the counter. While the sales clerk rang them up, I looked at the label again. I saw something I hadn't noticed before. There were little gold letters spelling out: *Dry clean only.*

Oops! Mom wasn't going to be too happy. But I'd just have to deal with it. After all, it was my life—my *new* life—not hers.

CHAPTER 7

This is incredible!" Vanessa exclaimed as she flitted around the cartwheel room. Her long, rose-colored skirt floated behind her. "This is the most wonderful room in the world!"

"Touchdown!" squawked Petey.

But Vanessa didn't notice.

Tara, Lauren, and Cassie had settled in on the pillows by Petey's cage. They were talking and munching on the chips, carrots, celery sticks, and dip that Mom had brought in.

I stood near Petey's cage, watching Vanessa go wild over the cartwheel room. I'd decided to let myself have three carrot sticks for a snack. I tried to nibble slowly. It wasn't easy.

Suddenly Cassie popped up from her pillow. She ran over to the barre and faced Vanessa. Whatever Vanessa did, Cassie did it, too. They reminded me of Lucy and Harpo Marx on "I Love Lucy"!

Then Vanessa raised a leg from the side of her body. Cassie did, too.

When her leg reached ear-level, Cassie let out a yelp.

"That's it for me!" she exclaimed, lowering her leg.

But Vanessa's leg just kept going. At last her foot was way up over her head. She held it there as if it were no big deal.

"Hi, guys! Hi, Tara!" cried Missy, running in. She'd spent the day over at her friend Tiffany's house.

"Hey, Missy!" said Tara. "Come sit over here by me."

"Who's *that?"* asked Missy, staring at Vanessa. She still held her foot up over her head.

"That's Vanessa," I said. "Vanessa, this is Missy."

"Wow," said Missy. Then she dashed off.

"Patti, put on that tape you bought!" Vanessa said. She seemed so excited. "Can you? Please? Please?"

"Sure!" I said. As the piano music started, Vanessa kicked off her shoes. She began bending and stretching at the barre.

I kicked off my shoes, too. I stood behind Vanessa, holding the barre. I tried to copy just what Vanessa did.

"I'm back!" Missy yelled. One look and I knew what she'd been up to. She'd been digging around in her dress-up bin, her closet, and *my* closet. She had on one of my T-shirts. A pale pink scarf was tied around her middle. Missy had put together her idea of Vanessa's outfit.

I glanced over at Tara. She looked a little bit hurt. After all, Missy usually copied what *she* wore!

Missy joined us at the barre. Then Lauren did, too. The four of us followed Vanessa for a long time.

Leaning on her pillows, Tara just watched. As she watched, she stuffed chip after chip into her mouth.

"Hay, Laur!" she said at last. "When did you learn ballet?"

"In gymnastics," Lauren said. "We took a class once a week."

Tara stood up, brushing crumbs from her hands. Suddenly she started galumphing around the studio like an elephant!

"Tara!" I cried. "What are you doing?"

"Ballet!" shrieked Tara. She circled the room, making giant flapping motions with her arms. She crossed her eyes.

"Stop it!" I yelled. She was ruining everything!

"Don't you get it?" Tara began limping then. She barely fluttered her arms. "I'm the swan! From *Swan Lake.* I'm dying!"

What was she trying to do, anyway? Embarrass me?

I stomped over to the tape player. I hit Stop. Suddenly the cartwheel room was very still. Caught in the midst of her death scene, Tara stuck out her tongue and collapsed on the floor.

Lauren and Cassie clapped.

"Oh, Patti, you can't call this the cartwheel room!" Vanessa sighed. She said it as if Tara's stupid dance had never happened.

"Why not?" asked Missy.

"Because," said Vanessa, "it's a wonderful ballet studio."

"So what should we call it?" Missy wanted to know.

"The studio," said Vanessa simply. "Just the studio."

I thought I heard Tara groan, "Give me a break!"

"I think you're right, Vanessa," I said loudly.

"Me, too," said Missy. "I hate that cartwheel room name. I'm going to tell Mom."

She took off, and we all sat down.

"Nice work on the chips, Tara," Lauren said, looking longingly at the empty bowl.

"Have a carrot," said Tara. "They're better for you anyway."

"Want one, Vanessa?" asked Lauren, passing the bowl of carrots.

"No, thanks," said Vanessa.

"But you haven't eaten a thing!" exclaimed Lauren. "I mean, you did so much exercise. It isn't good for you not to eat."

"Lauren," I said. "It's really not any of your business."

"But aren't you famished?" she asked Vanessa.

"I'm hungry," admitted Vanessa. "But I try not to snack."

"*Why?*" asked Lauren. "You're so thin."

"I gain weight from *looking* at an ice-cream carton," Vanessa said. "I have to watch what I eat every single minute." She looked over at me. "You know what I mean. Right, Patti?"

"Right," I said, glad to be in on one of Vanessa's secrets.

"That must be a total drag," said Tara.

"I'm used to it." Vanessa shrugged. "Ballet dancers *have* to be thin. Or male dancers can't lift them up. So . . . I stay thin."

Tara picked up a celery stick. She used it to scoop

up a huge glob of dip. She stuffed the whole thing into her mouth at once. Dip dripped down her chin. Was she *trying* to be piggy in front of Vanessa?

"Hey, I know," Tara said, wiping her chin with her sleeve. "Let's do some cheers for Vanessa!"

"No!" I said quickly.

Tara, Lauren, and Cassie all looked at me, surprised.

"I mean, I'm too tired to cheer," I said. It was true!

"Goll-durn it!" said Tara in her idea of a Texas accent. "I never thought I'd hear little ol' Patti Richardson say that!"

"Me, either," said Lauren.

"That makes three of us," said Cassie.

"Well, you heard it," I said grumpily. "I just don't feel like jumping around and yelling right now, okay?"

"What time is it?" Vanessa asked suddenly.

Cassie checked her watch. "Quarter to six."

"Oh, wow!" Vanessa turned to me. "I've got to get going." She stood up and slipped into her shoes.

"But . . . I thought you were staying for dinner," I said.

"You did?" She looked at me, tilting her head. "Sorry. My dad's picking me up at six at the Berkshire gate."

"But we were going to work on our report," I said. "Can't you call your dad? Can't you ask him to pick you up later?"

Vanessa shook her head. "I'm sure he's on his way." She bent down to pick up her ballet bag, never bending her knees. "Thanks anyway," she said. "Another time. Bye, everybody!"

I followed Vanessa to the front door. I watched as she ran down our sidewalk. Her feet hardly seemed to touch the ground.

Then I walked back into the ex-cartwheel room. Standing in the doorway, I felt my face getting warmer and warmer.

"Thanks a lot, Tara," I said. "Thanks a *whole* lot."

"You're welcome," said Tara. "Um . . . for what?"

"For driving Vanessa away," I said. "Why did you have to do that ridiculous dance?"

Tara shrugged. "I guess I thought it was funny."

"It *wasn't,"* I told her.

Tara shrugged. "It didn't seem to bother Vanessa."

"Well, it bothered me." I felt exhausted and close to tears. I plopped down on a cushion next to Lauren. "I just wanted us to have a good time together," I tried to explain. "I thought you all would like Vanessa."

"I like her, Patti," Lauren said. "She's really nice."

"Yeah," said Tara. "And that skirt of hers is fabulous!"

"I like her, too," added Cassie. "So what's the problem?"

"I don't know," I said. "Nothing, I guess. It just made me feel bad the way Vanessa left so suddenly."

"But Pah-ti, dah-link," said Tara in her Dracula voice. "Vee are steel here vit you!"

"True," I said. At one time that would have been

enough. But now all I really wanted to do was hang out with Vanessa.

"How about a fashion show?" Mom said when we'd finished the dishes that night. "Show us what you got at the mall today, Patti."

Tara, Lauren, and Cassie had gone home. My dad was down in the basement doing something with his fishing gear.

"Okay," I said. "Are you ever in for a surprise!"

"What surprise, Patti?" Missy said. She was sponging off the counters. "What? What? What?"

"Be right back!" I said. I zoomed up to my room and changed into my new outfit. Now, after dinner, the skirt was tighter than ever. Well, it wouldn't be for long. I slipped on my black flats.

I checked the mirror. I was maroon from my chin to my ankles. Remembering what Tara had said about a scarf or a belt, I headed for my closet. But hanger after hanger held nothing but solid color polo shirts and turtlenecks. Mom ordered them from the Lands' End or L.L. Bean catalog. Light blue. Navy blue. At last I came across a silver Navajo belt that Aunt Peggy had sent for Christmas. But when I belted the sweater, I looked sort of fat.

Flipping through hangers again, I stopped at my favorite summer dress. It was a Laura Ashley. It had a tiny blue flower print and a wide lace collar. That was me last summer, I thought. Now I'd put it in the hand-me-down box for Missy. This summer was going to see a brand-new Patti Richardson!

I brushed on a little blush and put on some lip gloss. Then I ran down stairs. Trying to feel elegant, I walked into the living room. Right in front of Mom, I twirled. "Tah-dah!"

"Wow, Patti!" exclaimed Missy. "You look like Vanessa!"

"Thanks, Missy!" I said. "Mom? What do you think?"

Mom had a strange expression on her face. "Well, Patti, honey," she said at last. "I *am* surprised! I was expecting school clothes. Just where are you planning to wear this dress?"

"It's not a dress. It's a sweater and skirt, see?" I lifted the bottom of the sweater a bit to show her. "And I could wear this to school. I was thinking of spending Grandma Ellie's Christmas money to get just the right shoes for it."

"What color do you call that dress, honey?" Mom asked.

"Maroon," I said.

"Maroon," she repeated. "I don't think that's going to coordinate with one single other thing in your wardrobe."

"That doesn't matter," I told her. "I'll just wear the skirt and sweater together. It's an outfit."

"And I'll bet it's going to bleed like crazy in the wash," Mom went on. "We'll have to be real, real careful what else we put into the machine with it."

"This, um, kind of has to go to the cleaners," I admitted.

"The cleaners!" exclaimed Mom. "Patti, do you—"

"I'll pay for it," I put in. "With my baby-sitting money."

Mom leaned back against the couch cushions. "Let's see what else you picked out, honey," she said.

"This is it, Mom," I said.

Her big blue eyes opened wide. "That's it? But what about school shirts? What about a new pair of jeans?"

"I didn't get anything else." I sat down on the edge of a wing chair opposite the couch. "I wanted something different," I tried to explain. "I'm tired of wearing the same kinds of clothes I've had my whole life. I want a new look."

"I know teenagers need to express their independence," Mom said, "but . . ." Her voice trailed off.

"But what?" I said.

"But . . . didn't they have it in another color?"

"Mom!" I sprang up from the chair. "I love this color!"

"Blue is your color, honey. Blue is such a *happy* color."

Just then Dad walked into the living room. *"Whoo-whee,* Patti-cakes!" he said. "Where are you off to, the prom?"

"No!" I said. I stomped inelegantly out of the living room.

As I ran up the stairs, I heard my dad's voice. "Sunny, honey?" he said. "Did I say something wrong?"

"No, Bill," I heard Mom answer. "But I guess I did."

CHAPTER 8

The next morning after church Mom and Dad dropped Missy and me back at home. Then they went on to a brunch. I was glad to baby-sit for Missy. I needed money for my dry-cleaning bills!

"What should we do?" asked Missy, following me upstairs.

"I have to do some homework," I told her. "Why don't you bring your Barbie coloring book and crayons into my room? You can color and I'll read about King George."

"Who's King George?" asked Missy.

"The King of England," I said. "And his cousin was Nicholas, the Tsar of Russia."

"Do you get to read about any queens?" asked Missy.

"Not for this report," I said.

"Too bad," said Missy. She ran off to get her things.

I looked at the three thick books stacked on my desk. Opening one of them was the *last* thing I wanted to do. But almost a week had gone by since Mr. Noonan assigned our reports. Vanessa and I hadn't written a single word! I *had* to crack those musty old books.

But first I decided to catch up on my Fat Book. I flopped down on my bed and started writing.

Sunday, March 23

Breakfast:

Toast—2 slices	Calories: 100	Fat: 0
Cantaloupe	Calories: 50	Fat: 0
Water	Calories: 0	Fat: 0
Total:	Calories: 150	Fat: 0

I loved writing in my Fat Book! I was keeping my calories and grams of fat way down. Best of all, when I weighed myself that morning, the scale said 103! I'd decided to keep going until I weighed 100. Writing down what I ate made me feel as if I were changing. Changing into a brand-new me.

"What are you doing, Patti?" Missy asked. She was standing beside my bed holding a stack of coloring books and her crayons.

"I'm keeping track of what I eat," I told her. "See?"

"Fat Book," Missy said, sounding out the title. I didn't think she could read most of what I'd written. I knew she didn't have a clue about calories or grams of fat. But I flipped through the pages anyway. She nodded as if she understood it all.

I got up then. I sat down at my desk.

"If I'm careful, can I color on your bed?" asked Missy.

"No," I told her. "Not on my white spread."

"What if I put Granny Nelly's quilt over it?"

"Good idea," I said. "You can't hurt that old thing."

"Don't you like it, Patti?"

"Not much," I said. "Listen, we can't talk any more, okay?"

"Okay," said Missy. "But Patti?"

"What?"

"If you don't like Granny Nelly's quilt, can I have it?"

"Sure, Missy," I said. "You can have it."

I was hungry. I had a slight headache. And I felt tired. I knew it was from not eating enough that morning. But I made myself settle down to work. I began reading the letters that George and Nicholas had written to each other. They were first cousins. They even looked alike. I could tell from their letters that they were good friends. Before they became King of England and Tsar of Russia, they traveled around Europe together. I took seven pages of notes for our report.

Just before noon the phone rang. I picked it up.

"Oh, Vanessa!" I was so happy to hear her voice! "Hi!"

"Hi," she said. "I have to tell you the weirdest thing."

"What?"

"Well, can I come over there and tell you?"

"Sure," I said. "When do you want to come?"

"Now," said Vanessa. "I'll bring some tapes and CDs. And I've got a leotard that's perfect for you. You can borrow it."

"Thanks!" I said. "And can we work on our report?"

"Great!" said Vanessa. "See you!"

Less than half an hour later our door chimes rang. Missy beat me to the door. There on our front porch stood Vanessa. She had her huge ballet bag slung over her shoulder. She walked inside saying, "Okay, here's the weird thing. Last night I had a dream about your ballet studio."

"What was the dream?" asked Missy as we followed Vanessa toward the studio.

"I dreamed it was in my house," Vanessa said. "That I danced in it for hours every day. And when Madame's school was closed, it didn't matter. I just went home and danced."

Inside the studio Vanessa peeled off her street clothes.

"Oh, Patti, here's the leotard I told you about," she said. She tossed it to me. It was royal blue. The top half was velvet.

"It's pretty," I said, holding it up. "But it looks *small.*"

"I think it'll fit you," Vanessa said. "It's big on me."

"Maybe it'll fit me!" Missy whispered.

Vanessa turned to her. "I've got a leotard that would fit you, Missy," she said. "I'll bring it to you tomorrow." Vanessa looked at me. "If it's okay for me to come over tomorrow."

"It's okay," said Missy quickly. "What color is it?"

"Bright red," said Vanessa. "You'll love it!"

"Oh, boy!" said Missy. "I love it already!"

Vanessa smiled. "So, Patti," she said. "Is it really okay?"

"Sure," I said. "But I thought you had a ballet class at Madame's on Monday's."

"Oh, I do," Vanessa said. "But it's over at five. I could come over here afterward. You know, for an hour or so."

"My cheerleading practice isn't over until five-thirty on Mondays."

"Oh," said Vanessa, frowning. "Well, could your Mom let me in or something?"

"I'll ask her," I said. "She'll probably say it's fine."

"Great! I'd just love it so much if I could dance over here after my ballet classes."

"You mean . . . like every day?" I asked.

"Well, if that's okay," said Vanessa. "Oh, thank you, Patti! Thank you! You know what this is like?"

"What?"

"It's like the dream I had last night is coming true!"

Vanessa put on a tape then. Piano music began playing. I ran upstairs to change. I didn't feel much like dancing. I still had a bit of a headache. But I put the leotard on anyway. It was made of stretchy material, so I got it on. But it *was* tight.

I walked back into the studio. Vanessa was in the middle of her barre exercises. She was already off in her own little world. So I didn't ask how she thought the leotard looked. Behind Vanessa stood Missy. She was trying to copy her moves.

For one whole hour we did barre exercises.

"I'm bored," Missy whined at last. "Can't we play something else now, Patti? How about Coach and Cheerleader?"

"No, Missy!" I tried to give my sister a look that meant *Don't talk about those silly games in front of Vanessa!*

She didn't get the message. "Well, how about Cheerleading Camp?" asked Missy. "You guys could be the counselors."

"Vanessa and I want to dance right now, Missy," I explained.

Missy sighed. "Okay, I'm going out to play with Spooky."

Spooky was a big white dog. He belonged to the Kellys, who lived next door. Drew Kelly was a seventh grader at PJHS. At the Lions' Dens, which are our school dances, he always asks me to dance. Tara teases me about liking him. And maybe I do. But I'll never admit it to her!

After Missy left, Vanessa and I kept practicing. The steps and turns Vanessa was doing were much too hard for me. So I just did the things I could. Over and over and over.

When the tape started playing for a third time, I said, "So, Vanessa? Are you ready to take a break?"

But Vanessa didn't even seem to hear me.

I tried to keep going. But I was too tired. And the

straps of Vanessa's leotard were cutting into my shoulders.

"Listen, Vanessa," I said, "I've got to check on Missy. Then I'll get our history books, okay? Maybe we should do a little work for our report. We've only got two weeks left."

Vanessa nodded, and I left her in the studio.

I changed back into my jeans and went out to find Missy. Drew came outside, and we talked to him for a while. Then I took Missy home. She said she was hungry, so I made her some soup.

"Aren't you eating any, Patti?" she asked.

"I'm not hungry," I told her, even though I really was. "I'll eat something later, with Vanessa."

I cleaned up the dishes. Then I gathered up our history books and my notebook. I lugged them into the studio. Missy came in with her coloring books.

Vanessa was practicing turns now. She looked hot. Strands of hair had come loose from her bun. They frizzed around her face.

"Ready to switch to history for a while?" I asked her.

Vanessa stopped for a moment. She caught her breath. "I just figured out what I was doing wrong on this turn," she said. "I've *got* to keep doing it the right way now. Otherwise, I'll lose it."

I sat down on the cushions. Vanessa really pushed herself in her dancing. I was sure someday she'd be a famous ballerina. Maybe, when we were older, she'd invite me to her opening night.

Pulling myself out of my daydream, I opened the

book on my lap. I looked up King George in the index of *The Last Days of the Tsar.* Then I started reading. During the Revolution, Nicholas and his wife, Alexandra, and their five children were taken prisoner. They were put into jail. Then they were taken by train out to the country. Wow! This was just what had happened to Vanessa's great-grandmother!

The Bolshevik soldiers were very cruel to the Tsar and his family. But the royal family never gave up hope. They believed that King George would rescue them. They were waiting for him to send a ship to take them to England.

Even though the book was old, the story inside was pretty interesting. I kept reading. I took six more pages of notes for our report.

As for Vanessa, she just kept dancing.

CHAPTER 9

Well, hello, Vanessa, honey!" Mom said when she and Daddy walked into the studio after their brunch. They sat down on the cushions beside Missy and me. We all watched Vanessa.

"Patti tells us that you've been going to dancing school for years and years," Dad said when the music ended.

Vanessa nodded. "I started taking ballet when I was four."

"That's just how old Patti and Missy were when they started cheering!" Mom exclaimed.

"Mom!" I moaned. "Um, listen, I want to ask you something."

"Shoot," said Mom.

"Would it be okay if Vanessa came over and danced in the studio in the afternoons?" I said.

Vanessa's eyes brightened. She clasped her hands together under her chin. "Would it?" she asked, bouncing on tiptoes.

"I don't see why not," said Mom. "My aerobics class meets from two to three o'clock. But after that, the cartwheel room—or the studio or whatever you're calling it—is yours!"

"Oh, thank you!" Vanessa exclaimed. She did a little leap of happiness. "Oh, you don't know what this means to me! Can I come tomorrow? A little after five?"

"Sure!" said Mom. "I think it's so wonderful that you want to dance in this room. It was truly made for dancing!"

"Hey," Dad said, "I've got an idea."

"Uh-oh," said Missy.

"I've never been to a ballet," Dad said. "And I was wondering—maybe you'd put on a little show for us some time."

"Dad!" I groaned. "Vanessa, you don't have to."

"Oh, I'd love to!" Vanessa spoke right up. "Really! It's a great idea. I *love* performing." Her eyes were shining. She turned to me. "Do it with me! Okay, Patti? Let's do it tonight!"

"Tonight?" Mom sounded surprised. "Well, all right."

Mom and Dad left the studio then. Missy said, "Can I be in your show, Vanessa? I have a dress-up bin. I have lots and lots of really cool costumes in it. Don't I, Patti?"

"You sure do," I said. And she did. Her friend Tiffany claimed it was the best collection of dress-up clothes in Paxton!

Vanessa said, "Great! But now let's figure out our dance."

"Um, maybe we should do a little work on our report first. I mean, just sort of get organized—decide who's doing what?"

"Yuck!" Vanessa wrinkled up her nose. "It can wait one more day, can't it, Patti?" Vanessa bounced on her toes again. "We have to figure out our show! Come on! Go put on some leotards!"

I ran upstairs. Maybe I should have chosen Emily for a history partner, I thought. But no. Then I would never have gotten to know Vanessa!

I changed back into the blue velvet leotard. Missy put on her black one. When we walked into the studio, Vanessa was playing another one of her classical music tapes. She was already making up a dance. She moved around the studio, trying out steps and mumbling to herself. Missy and I stretched out at the barre. We waited for her to tell us what to do. It took a long time.

"Okay, Patti," Vanessa said at last. "You and I are sister princesses. We're locked in a dungeon. We'll be executed at dawn. That's for the first part of the music," she explained. "Where it sounds sort of sad. We've been prisoners in the dungeon so long that we're slightly crazy."

"Am I a crazy princess sister, too?" asked Missy.

"No, you're our kitten," said Vanessa. "I'll show you how to do a *pas de chat.*"

Missy's eyes were wide. "What's that?" she asked.

"It means the 'step of the cat,' " Vanessa said, and

she demonstrated the springy little jump. "Now go over there"—she pointed to a corner of the studio—"and practice."

Missy scampered obediently over to the corner. She began doing the little jump over and over.

Vanessa turned back to me. "At the last minute," she said, "we escape. We run through the forest." She went on to describe how we found a house made of sugar, where a witch lived. It was a long, complicated story. She'd borrowed parts from many different fairy tales. She was totally into it.

The three of us worked on our dance until it was almost dinnertime. Then we ran upstairs. Vanessa lugged up her huge ballet bag. We looked through Missy's dress-up bin. I could tell Vanessa didn't think Missy's costumes were all that great.

"You could wear this," I offered, holding up a long pink-and-cream rayon nightgown. It had belonged to my grandma Ellie.

"I guess," said Vanessa. She changed into a light pink leotard from her ballet bag and slipped the nightgown over it.

I picked out a lime-green dress. I'd worn it the Halloween I was Scarlett O'Hara. It was sort of wrinkled. And the zipper was broken. Missy helped me pin it.

Vanessa and I wound scarves around our heads. Then I helped Missy put on white tights. Vanessa lent her a white leotard. It wasn't all that big on Missy. On her head Missy wore the ears from her last Halloween's pig costume.

When we were dressed, Vanessa rummaged in her

bag for her stage makeup. We made ourselves into very dramatic princesses. We had tons of blue eye-shadow and blush. With eyebrow pencil I drew whiskers on Missy's cheeks. Vanessa put on toe shoes.

"Okay, we're ready!" I called down the stairs to Mom and Dad. "Go sit in the studio! We'll make our entrance."

Vanessa led the way. I came next. Then Missy.

Mom and Dad clapped when they saw us. As Vanessa had instructed, Missy did her little cat step over to the stereo. She pressed the Start button on the CD player. We stood still as statues, waiting for our music to start.

Then we began our dance. Vanessa was the Rose Princess. She did most of the dancing. But then, she'd been studying ballet for years and years. So that made sense.

I was the Daisy Princess, the less important sister. Missy was our kitten, Buttercup. Most of the time Buttercup and I stood off to the side. Vanessa had shown us how to stand. With our heads tilted, we held our arms out slightly from our sides.

Even for our little audience of two, Vanessa danced her heart out. I could have watched her forever. I hardly even noticed the stiff neck I got from tilting my head.

Near the end of the dance the Rose Princess lay gracefully down on the floor. She fell sound asleep. As the last notes of the music sounded, she sat up. She stretched and looked around. This was supposed to show that the whole ballet had been a dream.

I wasn't sure whether Mom and Dad understood that or not. But anyway they clapped like crazy.

"More!" called Mom. *"Whoooie!* We want more!"

Why did Mom have to whoop like that? I glanced over at Vanessa. She didn't seem to mind. We did the dance again.

I'd never had so much fun! Being around Vanessa made me feel wonderful. She was so full of energy and excitement. Everything we did seemed like much more fun just because we did it together.

"Switch to your left!" Beth Ann directed us on Monday afternoon. The whole PJHS cheerleading squad was sitting on the gym floor. We had our legs out, stretching.

I leaned over my left leg and held my foot. I'd always been limber. But today I also felt thinner. That morning the scale had said 102! Being thinner felt good. Except for one thing. I was *hungry!* I'd only had an apple for lunch. Zero grams of fat. But how else could I get down to 100 pounds?

"No bouncing, Tara!" cautioned Steve Liu. He walked over to where Tara and I were stretching. Steve was a college student and our squad trainer. Tara had a major crush on him.

"Okay, Steve!" Tara called back. "No bouncing. Ever again!"

"So, Patti?" Tara said as Steve walked away. "What'd your mom think of your new outfit?"

"She wasn't crazy about it," I admitted.

"Too bad," said Tara. "Well, she probably wouldn't have liked the vinyl dress, either."

"You've got that right!" I said, laughing.

"Switch legs," Beth Ann said. "Now, while you're stretching, I'd like to go over the cheering schedule for the next few weeks. With both boys' and girls' basketball, track-and-field, and swimming to cheer for, we've got to split up."

Beth Ann asked for volunteers for each of the sports. When she said, "Girls' basketball," everybody put up a hand.

"You can't *all* cheer for the girls," Beth Ann said.

"Then pick the seventh graders!" Tara called out.

"Right!" cried Deesha. "We'll give our power to the Tower!"

Beth Ann laughed. "Okay! You asked for it. You've got it!"

All the seventh graders whooped up a storm. When practice started, we came together on a mat.

"This is going to be so cool!" said Michelle.

"Really!" said Kelsey. "I bet if we do our really hot stuff this Friday, we'll get picked to go to state with the team!"

We practiced all the basketball cheers we knew then. We did pony sits and double-based extensions and even Liberties.

"Okay, that's it for today," said Steve. "See you tomorrow."

"Bye, Stevie!" called Tara, waving.

Tara and I walked outside where Lauren and Cassie were waiting.

"I'm not walking home with you guys today," I told them. "Mom's picking me up."

"How come?" asked Tara. "I thought you were coming over."

Most days after practice the four of us walk into Paxton together. Lauren and Tara live right in town. Cassie goes to the radio station. That's where she does her homework. When her father finishes work, he drives her home. I usually go over to Lauren's or Tara's. Then Mom picks me up.

"I can't," I said. "Vanessa and I have to work on our history report."

I watched the three of them walk away. I felt a little lonely standing there on the curb.

That week Vanessa came over every day after her ballet class. She brought over leotards and tights and towels and toe shoes and changes of clothes. Plus lots of CDs and tapes. We made a little space in the studio where she kept everything.

Every day when I got home from cheerleading practice, I'd try to get Vanessa interested in working on history. But I could never get her out of the studio! I wasn't *that* worried. We still had more than a week to write our report. Once we got started I knew we could work fast.

Before Vanessa went home, we always weighed ourselves on my parents' scale. I went from 102 to 101! Vanessa only weighed 95 to begin with. On Thursday she was down to 94.

Thursday evening Mom came into the studio. "Missy

and I are going to the Paxton girls' basketball game tomorrow afternoon, Vanessa, honey," she said. "How'd you like to come with us?"

"Oh, no. Thanks anyway," Vanessa said.

"This could be your chance to see Patti cheer!" Mom added.

"Mom!" I said.

Vanessa just shook her head. Then she looked thoughtful. "So you won't be here tomorrow afternoon," she said.

"No," Mom said firmly. "We'll be at the game."

After Mom left the studio, Vanessa frowned. "I'll really miss coming over here. Um, what time's the game over?"

"Well, it starts at four," I said. "It'll probably last until around six or six-thirty."

Vanessa brightened. "Well, I could come over then, right?"

"Oh, okay," I said. "I'll call you when we get home."

Vanessa smiled. "Call me the second you walk in the door!"

"I will," I said. "Hey! You want to sleep over?"

"I'd *love* to!" Vanessa said, her eyes sparkling.

"One thing, Vanessa," I said. I tried to sound stern. "We've really, really got to get started on our report!"

"We will!" Vanessa said. "And *only* if we get some of our report done do we get to come in here and dance!"

"Okay," I said. "That's a good plan."

"Yes," said Vanessa. "Then we can dance all night long!"

CHAPTER 10

Hey, Lions!
Whadda ya say?
Tip that ball
Up, up and away!

All the seventh-grade cheerleaders whooped and hollered after our cheer. We'd been whooping and hollering for two hours! Kelsey had totally lost her voice. So Tara was cheering for her.

There were just six seconds left in the game. The Paxton Lions' girls' basketball phenoms were trouncing the Webster Wildcats! After a tie ball Jade Moyer and one of the Wildcats faced each other. When the referee tossed the ball, Jade tipped it up, up, and away—right into the waiting hands of the Tower. Liza pivoted, aimed, and fired. Bingo! The buzzer sounded. The game was over. We'd won, 94 to 78!

"All right!" I called. "Way to play, guys! Way to play!"

We walked over to say good-bye to the Wildcat cheerleaders. Then the seven of us headed for the girls' room.

The bathroom mirror showed me my bright red face. I pulled off my sweater. In just my tank top, I felt better. I took off my ring and my megaphone necklace and slipped them into my skirt pocket. Then I splashed cool water on my arms, face and neck.

"I am so pumped!" exclaimed Kelsey. "What a game!"

"Really!" said Michelle. She wiped her forehead with a paper towel. "I can't wait to get to Bingo's and devour a whole pizza."

"Just one more win, guys!" said Michelle. "And then it's on to the regionals!"

Lauren looked into the mirror. "Yikes!" she said. "Why didn't somebody tell me my bangs had gone ballistic?"

"Here," said Tara, slipping a handful of baby barrettes out of her pocket. "These'll help."

"No, thanks," Lauren said. "I'll stick to bobby pins." She began pinning back the loose strands of her hair. "I may not make it," she muttered. "I'm sick of letting my bangs grow out."

Deesha glanced over at me. "Patti, are you losing weight?"

"A little," I said, feeling happy that it showed.

Deesha raised her eyebrows. "Well, don't lose anymore, girl! You might dry up and blow away."

"I don't think so," I said. I blotted my face with a towel. I refastened my megaphone charm around my neck.

"Hey, Patti?" Cassie called from inside a stall. "Can I get a ride over to Bingo's with you?"

"Um, I'm not going," I called back.

"Patti!" exclaimed Lauren. "Why not?"

"Vanessa's coming over," I explained.

"So bring her to Bingo's," said Lauren. "Come on! It won't be any fun if you're not there!"

"I can't," I said. It was really hard to say no! "We've got tons of work to do for our history report," I added.

"Wow. You've been working so hard on that report," Lauren said. "I hope you get an A plus."

"Me, too," I said.

Lauren gave me a hug. "We'll miss you."

"See you, guys!" I made myself walk out of the girls' room. But right outside the door I paused. My ring. Had I left it on the sink? I checked my pockets. Just as my fingers found my ring, I heard Tara's voice loud and clear.

"You know," she said, "I think it would be good for Patti to lose some more weight."

I slipped on my ring. But I was too stunned to move.

"What! She's too skinny now!" I heard Lauren exclaim.

"I wish she'd lose ninety pounds," Tara went on. "Ninety pounds of Vanessa."

I couldn't believe my ears! I whirled around. I stomped furiously back into the bathroom.

"Tara!" I practically shouted. "I heard that! How could you say that?"

The room grew totally quiet. I stood there, my hands on my hips. My face felt boiling hot. I waited for an answer.

"Come on." Tara jerked her head in the direction of the door. "We need to talk."

I followed her out of the girls' room and down the hall. By a drinking fountain Tara turned to face me. For a moment neither of us spoke.

"I said what I did because I do wish it," Tara said at last. "I'm sorry," she added. "It was mean. I shouldn't have said it."

"You're right," I said. "I thought you were my friend."

"I am!" Tara said.

"Friends don't talk about their friends behind their backs," I pointed out.

"I said I was sorry. And I am. Please don't be mad at me."

I let out a long breath. Already I didn't feel quite so mad.

"I think I know why you said that," I told Tara. "It's because Vanessa and I have gotten to be really good friends. Maybe you feel left out."

Tara looked thoughtful. "Maybe," she said. "But that's not the only reason. I know you're a good friend to Vanessa." She looked down at the floor. "But I don't think Vanessa's a very good friend to you."

"Yes, she is!" I insisted. "She's a wonderful friend! We have so much fun together."

Tara shrugged. "Just be careful. Okay, Patti?"

"Of what?"

"I don't know. Just do." With that, Tara gave me a wave. Then she walked slowly back down the hall.

I felt bad, watching her go. Tara had been my first friend in Paxton. This mean girl, Darcy Lewis, had made fun of me the first day of cheerleading clinic. And Tara had told her off. Tara had practically saved my life!

But now she was jealous. That's what made her talk that way in the girls' room. Jealous that I had another friend. Jealous that I was becoming thin and elegant. Jealous that I was becoming just like Vanessa.

"No, thank you," said Vanessa at dinner that night in our dining room. She passed me the spare ribs. I didn't take one, either.

"Well, how about some of Sunny's famous creamy mashed potatoes?" Dad asked Vanessa.

"No," Vanessa said. "I'll just have some salad."

I wished I'd talked to Mom about what she was cooking for dinner. No wonder it was taking so long for me to lose weight! Mom probably got her recipes from the *All Fatty Foods Cookbook!*

"Salad," said Mom, passing Vanessa the big wooden bowl. "Here you go, honey. Ranch dressing?"

"No," said Vanessa. "I'd like lemon juice. That's what I usually put on my salad."

"Lemons are in a bowl on the counter," Mom said. "Patti, honey, you want to squeeze a little lemon juice for your guest?"

"Okay," I said, getting up. "I'll just have salad, too."

"Me, three!" called Missy.

"Oh, no, you don't, Melissa," Mom said. "Oh, no, you don't."

I ate just what Vanessa ate for dinner that night: salad with lemon juice. I knew Mom wouldn't give me a hard time about not eating. Not in front of company.

"Patti's told us some of the stories about your ancestors escaping during the Russian Revolution, Vanessa," Dad said as we ate. "They sure had some hard times. Who told you the stories?"

"My mother," Vanessa said. "My grandfather told them to her. He says we must never forget that royal blood runs in our veins."

Having Vanessa over for dinner was so interesting. It made me forget all about Tara and her jealousy.

"Is it red?" Missy whispered to me.

"Is what red?" I whispered back.

"Royal blood."

I nodded. "It means that Vanessa is related to the royal family of Russia."

"What about us?" Missy asked Dad. "What kind of blood do we have in our veins?"

"Not royal blood," said Dad. "But we do have some colorful ancestors like my great-uncle Charlie. He was really something."

Cool, I thought. I didn't just have plain old Nelly Keller. I had an ancestor who was really something!

"What did Great-Uncle Charlie do?" asked Missy.

"Great-Uncle Charlie was a wildcatter," Dad said.

"He was a *cat?*" asked Missy.

"He was an oil-well driller," Dad went on. "But he didn't drill wells for big oil companies. He and his partner, Snake-eye Simpson, went out on their own."

"He was partners with someone named Snake-eye?" I asked. I started getting a little bit worried about my ancestor.

"Yep," said Dad. "Charlie and Snake-eye drilled wells in fields where nobody thought there was any oil at all."

"Did they find oil?" asked Missy.

"Hold your horses," said Dad. "I'm getting to that. Charlie and Snake-eye went out to west Texas. They went out to a field that other wildcatters had given up on. Everybody said they were darned fools. But Charlie and Snake-eye didn't listen. They just rolled up their sleeves and got to work. They drilled three deep holes in the ground." Dad looked around at all of us. "You know what they called those three holes in the ground, don't you?"

We all shook our heads.

"Well, well, well." Dad grinned.

"Dad!" I groaned. "That was a *joke?*"

"Oh, Bill!" Mom exclaimed, laughing. "That was *low.*"

"You mean we don't really have a Great-Uncle Charlie?" Missy asked.

"Oh, we do," said Dad. "And he was a wildcatter."

"Did he have a partner named Snake-eye?" asked Missy.

"Well . . ." Dad said. "Maybe not Snake-eye."

"Who's for some chocolate cake?" Mom asked.

"No, thank you," said Vanessa.

"No, thanks, Mom," I said. "May we please be excused?" I added. "We really need to get started on our history report."

"You're excused," Mom said.

"May I please be excused?" asked Missy.

"If you don't want any chocolate cake," Mom said.

Missy thought for a couple of seconds. "I'll be excused after my cake," she said.

I picked up my dishes and carried them into the kitchen.

Vanessa stood up from the table. "I'll be in your room," she said to me and walked toward the stairs.

"How come Vanessa doesn't carry her plate in?" asked Missy.

"Missy! Shhhh!" Quickly I picked up Vanessa's dishes.

"Maybe she doesn't do it at her house," Mom said softly.

"I know why," Missy said. "She has royal blood in her veins!"

CHAPTER 11

Sorry about my dad's sense of humor," I said when I walked into my bedroom. Vanessa was lying on my bed. She was looking at my *Seventeen.* She just kept turning the pages of the magazine.

I unzipped my backpack. I pulled out my history notebook and two pens. *The Letters of Nicholas and George, The Last Days of The Tsar,* and *A King's Story* were stacked on my desk.

"So," I said, "maybe we should make an outline. Then we'll know how much work we have to do."

"Do you like this bikini?" Vanessa turned the magazine to me.

The picture on the page showed a super-thin model sitting on a diving board wearing a skimpy flower-print swimsuit.

"On her it's okay," I said. "But my mom would have a fit if I wanted to buy a suit like that."

"Mine, too," said Vanessa.

"Yeah? What's your mom like, anyway?" I asked.

"My mother is tall and thin," said Vanessa. "She and my father go out almost every night. My mother piles her long black hair on top of her head. She wears beautiful gowns, all covered with sequins and pearls. And her perfume smells of roses."

"Wow!" I breathed. Vanessa spoke about her mother almost the way she did when she told stories of her ancestors.

"What about your father?" I asked.

"My father is as handsome as a movie star," said Vanessa. "When he and my mother go out, he slicks back his dark hair. He wears a tuxedo with a stiff white shirt and a crimson cummerbund."

It was hard to picture people as elegant as Mr. and Mrs. Ivanova even living in Paxton!

"Your parents sound pretty different from mine!" I said.

Vanessa laughed. "They are! Completely different!"

"What's your house like?" I asked.

"It's big," Vanessa said. "It's like a palace, really."

"Yeah?" I said. "That's what Tara always says about Cassie's house. She calls it Copeland Castle." I frowned then, remembering what else Tara had said. "Where is your house?" I asked Vanessa.

"On the far side of the lake," she said. "So . . ." She sat up. "I guess we should start doing our history. I forgot to bring my notebook. You have some paper or something?"

"My mom has notebook paper. I'll go get you some."

Vanessa flopped down across my bed again, looking at *Seventeen*. I hurried downstairs. When I walked into the kitchen, Dad was putting dishes into the dishwasher. Mom was sitting at her desk. Missy was sponging off the counters.

"Patti, honey!" Mom exclaimed when she saw me. "We were proud of you tonight at dinner!"

"You were?" I said.

"You are a truly polite and considerate hostess," Mom said.

What was she talking about? I wondered.

"That was so sweet of you," Mom continued. "Eating just what Vanessa ate to make her feel comfortable at our house. Get Patti her plate, Bill," Mom added. She gave me a wink. "We had a hunch you'd be back down to get a little something."

Dad opened the oven and brought out a dinner plate loaded with ribs, mashed potatoes, and green beans. "Here you go, Patti-cakes," he said. "Nice and hot."

I shook my head. "No, really," I said. "I had my dinner. I just came down to get some notebook paper."

"But you must be famished," Mom said, placing the plate on the counter. "Here, sit down and eat. Being polite is one thing. But you don't have to go to sleep hungry!"

"But I didn't eat just salad to be polite," I tried to explain. "I don't want to eat so much anymore."

Mom put her hands on her hips. "Well, why in the world not?"

"Because I'm trying to control my weight," I told her. I could tell my face was turning red.

"Your *weight?"* Mom said.

"You don't think you're overweight, do you, Patti-cakes?" Dad said.

"I just want to lose a couple of pounds," I said. "I don't want to eat foods with so much fat in them."

"For your information, Patrice Richardson, no one in our family has ever had a weight problem," Mom said. "You're much too active to cut down on what you eat. You need good food to give you energy!"

"Can we talk about this later, please? I came down here to get paper. May I have some?"

Mom opened the closet where she kept paper supplies.

"Here." She handed me a stack of paper. "Now, when you and Vanessa get hungry, Patti, honey, for heavens' sake come down here and fix yourselves something to eat."

I ran back upstairs then. And guess what? Vanessa and I actually started working on our history report! We agreed on what to do. I'd report on George and Nicholas as young men. And she'd report on them during the Russian Revolution. We didn't get too far. But this was real progress!

On Saturday morning Mom drove Vanessa and me to ballet class. I tried my hardest on my leaps. And it paid off!

At the end of class Madame nodded at me. "Good," she said.

At cheerleading practice, a little *good* wouldn't

mean very much. But at ballet, *good* was about as good as it got.

Except for Vanessa. After she leaped across the studio, Madame said, "Excellent, Vanessa! Excellent!"

Vanessa had a private lesson with Madame that afternoon. So after my class, I met Cassie and Lauren at the mall. I wasn't exactly sorry when they told me that Tara had gone to Chicago. She was spending the weekend with her dad, her stepmother, and her little sister, Lucy.

So Tara wasn't around when I picked out tights and shoes to go with my new outfit. I didn't need her! For me, the tights were pretty wild. They were plaid—deep maroon with light maroon and black. They were just like a pair I'd seen in *Seventeen.* I also got a pair of black patent-leather shoes. They had very pointy toes and little laces. I couldn't wait to wear them!

But I had to. That was the deal I'd made with myself. I couldn't go to school dressed as the new me until I got down to 100 pounds.

At school on Monday and Tuesday I avoided Tara. I didn't make a big deal out of it. At lunch I ate my apple and slice of bread with Emily and some girls from my computer class. They didn't nag me about eating more! And at cheerleading practice I just got into groups with other girls. I wasn't really mad at Tara. For some reason I just didn't feel like talking to her.

Before dinner on Tuesday I stepped on the scale. To my surprise, the needle pointed to 100 pounds!

"Whoopie!" I shouted. "I did it! I did it!" I zoomed down the hallway.

Missy poked her head out of her room. "Did what, Patti?"

"I weigh exactly one hundred pounds!" I told her.

My sister followed me into my room. She watched me take the maroon sweater out of my drawer. I laid it carefully across the foot of my bed. Then I took the silky chiffon skirt out of my closet. I laid it next to my sweater. Tomorrow I'd wear my new outfit to school. Tomorrow, April 2nd, was going to be NEW ME DAY!

"This is beautiful, Patti," Missy said. She stroked the chiffon skirt. "It's just like what Vanessa wears."

"I hope your hands are clean," I said.

"They are," Missy assured me. "I only petted Spooky a little bit. And he had a bath last week."

"Yuck, Missy. I don't want to smell like dog! If you touch my clothes, you have to wash your hands."

Next I laid out my new tights and shoes.

"Patti?" Missy said. "When your shoes aren't new anymore, will you let me wear them?"

"Sure," I said. "But they won't fit you for years."

"That's okay," she said. "I can stuff them for Halloween."

"Halloween!" I exclaimed.

"Yes," said Missy. "For witch shoes."

"For your information, Melissa, these shoes are very fashionable," I said. "When you're older, you'll understand."

"Okay," said Missy.

She sat down then. She began looking at my Fat Book. I just stared at my new clothes. I loved them! I couldn't wait to wear them tomorrow. I couldn't wait to show off the brand-new me.

I'd just climbed into bed that night when the phone rang.

"Is it my imagination?" Tara said. "Or have you been trying not to be around me lately?"

"It's not your imagination," I admitted.

"I didn't think so," she said.

For a moment neither of us spoke. Then Tara said, "I just want you to be careful, Patti."

"You already said that."

"I know. But Vanessa's into starving herself. And now you—"

"She isn't starving," I interrupted Tara. "Besides, she told you why she doesn't eat much. Ballet dancers have to be light."

"I think she has an eating problem," Tara said. "And I don't want you to have one, too."

"I feel good a few pounds lighter," I told her. "I feel great! Don't worry! I know what I'm doing."

"But I am worried," said Tara. "And there's another reason."

"What?"

"Well, every time I talk to you, Vanessa's over at your house. She's always in the cartwheel room—excuse me, the *studio.*"

"So what? She loves to dance. We happen to have a ballet studio. What's the big deal?"

"It just seems so one-sided," Tara explained. "How

come your good friend Vanessa never asks you over to *her* house?"

"Oh, Tara. You don't understand. You don't even want to."

"You know what I think? I think Vanessa's using you, Patti."

"What?" I exclaimed. "She is not!"

"Well, I think she is. Now you know." She was quiet for a few seconds. "Now you're really going to avoid me at school."

"This . . . this just isn't any of your business," I told her.

"I know," she said. "But you're my friend. And I just can't stand what Vanessa's doing. So, that's all. Bye, Patti."

We hung up then. But it was a long time before I fell asleep. I just lay there in the dark, thinking: *What if Tara's right?*

CHAPTER 12

When I woke up on Wednesday morning, all my nighttime worries seemed silly. I got dressed in my new outfit. I put on a little bit of blush and lipstick. Walking into school, I made a slight rustling sound. I felt so elegant!

The first person I saw in the hallway was Drew Kelly. He was standing with his football buddies, T.D. and Justin.

"Hi, Drew," said the new me. I walked toward him.

"Hi," Drew said.

"What's with the weird clothes?" Justin muttered.

I gave a little shrug. "Just ready for a change, I guess."

"Hey, Patti?" T.D. said. "You know what?"

"What?" I said.

"*Yesterday* was April Fools' Day!"

All three boys started laughing like crazy then.

My face turned beet red. I just walked by them. At that moment I really, really, really hated boys. What did they know about fashion, anyway? Nothing, that's what. Absolutely nothing.

As the day went on, my new clothes got lots of different reactions. In my English class Zoe Kimmel said at first she thought I was a student teacher. Michelle Bostick asked me if I was in a play. Kiri Kelly, who edits the school newspaper, stopped me in the hall. She asked me where I got the cool tights. The *yes* votes were running ahead of the *no* votes all morning.

At lunch I got in line for the salad bar. The hot lunch was creamed tuna. So the salad bar line was pretty long. The other seventh-grade cheerleaders got into line behind me. I hadn't seen most of them all morning. I tried not to look at Tara.

"Hmmm," Cassie said. She studied me for a minute. "Your new look is going to take some getting used to."

"I like your old look, Patti," Lauren said. *"For sure."*

"Come on, guys!" Tara said. "Lighten up! Give Patti a little credit for venturing into the world of cutting-edge style!"

"Is that a compliment?" I asked Deesha.

"I don't think so," she answered.

"I'd die for the shoes," said Tara. I had to give her credit. She was trying to be nice. "What size are they?"

"Seven."

"Hey, I'm barely an eight! I bet I could squeeze into them. I mean, if you'd let me borrow them sometime." She leaned over and whispered, "But kill the tights."

"Really?" I said. "Kiri Kelly liked them."

"I rest my case," said Tara. "The tights die."

"Is that all you're eating, Patti?" said Lauren as I put an apple on my tray.

"I'm not that hungry," I said. And this time I wasn't lying. For a couple of days now, I'd hardly eaten at all. But I didn't feel hungry. Ever. It was like my body had adjusted to less food. Now I couldn't even think of anything like creamed tuna without feeling sort of sick.

"Oh, sure," said Lauren. "You're not hungry at all."

"Psst! Patti!" someone called.

I looked around. It was Vanessa. She was standing outside the cafeteria door. When I looked over at her, she waved for me to come over. This was the first time I'd seen her all day.

"What does she want?" Cassie asked.

I was sure she wanted to tell me how great my new outfit looked.

"Guess I'll go find out," I said.

"Don't get out of line, Patti," warned Lauren. "You'll never have time to eat if you do."

"And you better eat, Patti," said Tara.

"Oh, I'll get something from the juice machine," I snapped. I cut out of line. I left my tray sitting on the metal rails.

"Come with me," Vanessa whispered as I walked toward her.

"Hold it," I said. "Aren't you going to say anything about my outfit?" I gave a little twirl.

"Oh, it looks good!" she exclaimed. "Really. So come on!"

"Where?" I said, already following her down the hallway.

She kept walking until we were right outside the nurse's office. A metal sign on the door said MS. BERGMAN, R.N. I'd never been to the nurse's office before.

"Are you sick?" I asked.

"No," Vanessa whispered. "Ms. Bergman just went to lunch. Let's sneak into her office and weigh ourselves."

"But we weigh ourselves at my house practically every day."

"No offense, Patti," said Vanessa. "But your scale isn't exactly state-of-the-art. Ms. Bergman's is one of those balance scales. Totally accurate. So let's go see what we *really* weigh."

"Okay," I said. "But what if we get caught?"

Vanessa made a funny face. "What are they going to do, kick us out of school?"

I giggled nervously. Vanessa opened the door to the nurse's office. I followed her inside.

An eighth-grade boy was sitting at Ms. Bergman's desk. He looked up from his book. "May I help you?" he said.

Vanessa wasn't the least bit flustered. "Oh, hi!" she said. She flashed him her biggest smile. "I was in here earlier. I had a headache. And now I can't find my

English book." She pointed to the back room. "Can I see if I left it here?"

"Okay," hc said.

"Thanks!" she said, and we walked back. The room was furnished with another desk and four cots. Each cot had a curtain that could be drawn around it. Against the far wall stood the official scale.

"I'll go first," Vanessa offered. She kicked off her shoes and stepped up onto the platform. She moved the large weight to 50 pounds. Then she began tapping the smaller weight with her finger. The scale finally balanced between forty and forty-one pounds.

"Ninety and a half," she said, hopping off. "Good!"

"You weigh less on this scale than on ours," I said.

"Hurry up, Patti," Vanessa whispered. Then in a loud voice, she added, "Did you find the book under that bed?"

After pulling off my shoes and stepping onto the scale, I pushed the bottom weight to 100. Then I hit the top weight all the way down to the left. But even on zero, it was too heavy.

"Hey!" I whispered. "This says I'm under a hundred pounds!"

I put big weight back to fifty. I tapped the small one until it balanced at forty-eight.

"Ninety-eight!" I whispered.

Vanessa pushed both weights back to zero and we walked out to the front room.

"It's not here," she said to the boy at the desk. "But thanks for letting us look."

The boy nodded and went back to reading.

Out in the hallway Vanessa squeezed my arm. "Ninety-eight!" she exclaimed. "That should inspire you."

"Yeah," I said. I was still sort of shocked to find out I weighed in the nineties. "But . . . what do you mean, inspire me?"

"You know," said Vanessa. "To keep going!"

"Keep going?" I asked. The bell to end my lunch period rang. "You mean to lose *more?*"

"Sure!" Vanessa smiled. "Keep going. Maybe you'll catch up with me. Then we'll weigh exactly the same!" She gave my arm another squeeze. "I can't wait to get to your house today, Patti!" Then she took off down the hallway.

I walked slowly toward my computer classroom. Vanessa weighed ninety and a half. I was down to ninety-eight. Losing weight hadn't been *that* hard. I wondered if I could lose seven and a half more pounds. If I did, then I'd really be just like Vanessa.

CHAPTER 13

Ouch! I limped into the locker room to change for cheerleading practice that afternoon. My new shoes had rubbed blisters on both my baby toes. And my heels. My skirt still pinched at the waist. At this point I was ready to vote *no* on my new outfit.

I never had made it back to the juice machine. I hadn't eaten anything at all since breakfast—half a slice of toast. I wasn't hungry. But as I put on my sweatsuit, I felt strangely light-headed. I ran my warm-up laps around the track anyway. Pretty soon the dizzy feeling went away. Then I started feeling really great! As I ran, I forgot all about my blisters. I felt as if I could run forever! I ran six laps in the time everyone else ran four. Then I caught up with a clump of seventh graders walking toward the gym.

"I am so psyched to cheer at the district finals on Friday," Lauren was saying. "I hope Beth Ann says we can do it."

"I hear Hazelwood has a pretty good team," said Kelsey.

"But we can beat them," Tara said.

"Seventh graders!" Beth Ann called after we stretched out. "Steve and I would like to meet with you on the blue mat."

We darted looks at one another. We were sure they were going to tell us we could cheer for the girls at Friday's big game. It was a night game, too. That always made it more exciting.

"Can we see your basketball cheers?" said Steve.

Six of us lined up. Tara stood on the sidelines.

" 'We're on top' " Michelle said. "Ready, *and!*"

Lions! Let's score!
Two points! Two more!
We're ready! We're on top!

On the word *ready,* Deesha and I jumped to face each other, our knees bent. Keeping our elbows pressed close to our bodies, we held out our hands. Standing behind us, Kelsey popped Cassie up. Deesha and I grabbed her feet.

Lion spirit . . .

Suddenly I felt light-headed again. I lost the count. Deesha pushed Cassie's right foot up. But I was still holding her left foot down close to my chest.

"Hey!" Cassie yelled. "Help!"

Steve, Beth Ann, and Tara all rushed forward. Steve caught Cassie just before she hit the mat. Behind me, Kelsey still chanted the last line of the cheer:

will never drop!

But Cassie *had* dropped! My heart pounded. I felt dizzy. Sick to my stomach. Everything turned blurry. I felt my legs turn to rubber. The last thing I remember seeing was the bright blue mat.

I opened my eyes. Where was I? Then I saw the scale. Ms. Bergman's office! I remember thinking it was funny. I'd never been to the nurse's office. Now I was there twice in one day.

"Patti?" Beth Ann said. "Can you hear me?"

"Uh-huh," I said.

"Okay, sit up slowly," she said. "That's it."

I sat up on the cot, blinking. Dark blotches swam in front of my eyes. Then it all came back to me. The cheer. Cassie . . .

"How's Cassie?" I said.

"She's not too happy," Beth Ann said. "But she's not hurt."

I let out a long breath and closed my eyes again.

"Take a sip of this." Beth Ann put a straw to my mouth. I sipped. Ginger ale, it tasted like. "A few swallows and you'll start feeling better."

She was right. A minute later the blotches disappeared.

"I guess I fainted," I said.

"You did," said Beth Ann. "You can't live on air, you know, Patti. You need good nutritious food to fuel your body."

She sounded like my mom!

"I understand you've been dieting."

"A little bit." I looked up at her. "Tara told you, didn't she?"

"That doesn't matter," Beth Ann said.

Well, it did to me!

"Besides," Beth Ann went on, "I would have figured it out today. You can't stop eating and still do all the things you do—like cheerleading."

I nodded as I finished the ginger ale.

"I phoned your mother," Beth Ann went on. "I didn't reach her. But I left a message on her machine. I said that I want to talk to her."

I bit my lip. What would Mom think?

"What happened this afternoon is serious," Beth Ann said.

"I know."

"You need to stop dieting," Beth Ann continued. "And until I'm sure that you have, I'm suspending you from the squad."

I'm Patti Richardson, I thought as I lay there on that cot. Beth Ann had drawn the curtain around it. *I've been a cheerleader since I was four years old. I'm a Paxton cheerleader.*

No. That wasn't right. I was a *suspended* Paxton cheerleader.

Somewhere in the background I heard a phone ring. It was my mom. She and Beth Ann talked a while. Then Beth Ann came over to me. She pulled aside the curtain.

"Your mother will be here in about ten minutes," she said.

"Did you tell her what happened?" I asked.

"Yes," said Beth Ann. "It's part of my job to communicate problems to parents."

What was Mom going to think? What was she going to say?

"What about the other girls on the squad?" I asked. "Do they have to know that I'm . . ." I couldn't say the word *suspended.*

Beth Ann shook her head. "I'll just say you're taking a little time off," she said.

As if they wouldn't know what that meant!

"Patti, I'd like to see how much you weigh now." Beth Ann nodded her head in the direction of the scale.

"Ninety-eight," I said in a small voice. I walked shakily over to the scale and adjusted the weights.

"What did you weigh a month ago?"

"One-hundred five. I didn't mean to lose so much," I tried to explain as I stepped down.

"You overdid it." She put an arm around my shoulders. "Let's see you get up to one-hundred pounds again. Then I'll put you back on the squad—but only if you promise to keep gaining." She gave me a little squeeze. "Don't worry if it takes you a while to get your old appetite back. It'll come."

I nodded. But I wasn't sure how I felt about gaining weight. Tears gathered in my eyes.

"I don't like doing this," Beth Ann told me. "But right now you're not in any shape to be a member of a cheerleading squad. It's too dangerous for you. And for the other cheerleaders. They need to be able to trust you as a stunt partner."

I was sobbing by the time she finished. I threw myself down on the cot and cried into the pillow.

After a while Mom walked into the nurse's office. She chatted with Beth Ann. I heard her say, "We'll get this all straightened out." Then she peeked around the curtain. "Hi, Patti, honey," she said. "Let's go home."

Mom had my backpack slung over her shoulder. I walked beside her down the empty hallway. We left through the front door of the school. I was glad. I couldn't have walked through the gym!

Mom didn't say much on the ride home. She could tell I was super upset. All she said was, "You feel okay now, honey?"

"I'm not going to faint, if that's what you mean."

"I'll fix you a little snack when we get home," she said. "It'll make you feel better."

"Okay." We pulled into the driveway. "Is Vanessa here?"

"Yep," Mom said. "She's in the studio, dancing."

"Mom?" I said suddenly. "Do you think Vanessa's a good friend?"

For a few seconds, Mom didn't say anything. Then she reached over and stroked my hair. "Patti, honey," she said, "that's not something I can tell you. That's something you'll have to figure out for yourself."

CHAPTER 14

I walked into the studio. One of Vanessa's classical music tapes was playing. Vanessa was standing at the barre. Her left leg was extended out to the side. Slowly she bent her right knee and brought her left foot back behind her. She was totally focused on what she was doing. She didn't even know I'd come into the room.

"Kill 'em!" Petey cried as I tiptoed past his cage.

I sat down on a pillow. I bit a rough edge off a fingernail.

Then I noticed Missy. She was standing beside Vanessa at the barre. She had on Vanessa's bright red leotard. She'd wrapped a gauzy scarf around her middle. She was trying her hardest to do what Vanessa did. *That's exactly what I've been doing,* I thought.

Mom came in. She brought me a tray with carrot sticks, chips, and guacamole. And a tall glass of lemonade. I tried to munch on a carrot stick. But I couldn't eat much.

When the piece of music ended, Missy said, "Hi, Patti!"

Vanessa bent down and picked up a towel and wiped her face. "What time is it?" she asked.

"About five," I said.

Vanessa nodded. "I have time to do this barre once more."

"Vanessa?" I said as she walked over to the tape player.

"Hmmm?" She pressed the Rewind button.

"I got suspended from the cheerleading squad," I said.

"Patti!" Missy exclaimed. She came running over. She threw her arms around me and didn't let go.

Vanessa kept her eyes on the tape player. She didn't say anything. When the counter reached 000, she pressed Stop.

Then she hurried over to me. "What happened?" she asked.

I explained about Cassie's fall. And how it was my fault. I started crying again. Then Missy started crying, too.

"That's awful, Patti," Vanessa said. "But you know what?"

"What?" I said, wiping my eyes with the end of my sleeve.

"Now you can take more ballet classes!" She smiled. "Listen, my mom's meeting me at the gate at five-thirty. I've got to go through this barre one more time." She ran over to the tape player. "One more time."

Missy sat beside me on the pillow. We watched Vanessa. The whole time Missy held my hand. That made me feel a bit better.

But Vanessa had made me feel worse. She didn't seem to care that I'd been kicked off the squad. Of course I hadn't talked about cheerleading around her. Not much. Maybe she didn't understand how important it was to me. And maybe until today, I didn't understand, either.

When Vanessa finished, she started tossing everything into her ballet bag—all the clothes and towels and ballet shoes she'd left at our house for two weeks. Even all her tapes and CDs.

"How come you're taking your music?" Missy asked her.

"My mom wants me to," Vanessa said. "She likes to keep track of things. And, oh, she wants me to get my leotards back, too."

"I'll wash them tonight," I told her. "I'll give them to you tomorrow."

"No," she said. "I better take them now."

I turned and stomped up to my room. Missy followed me. Why did Vanessa have to have her stupid leotards right this minute? Would it kill her to wait one day?

"Here," I said, handing her the two wadded-up leotards. She stuffed them into her ballet bag. I walked her to the door.

"See you tomorrow," I said in a tired voice. "I guess we'll have to spend all weekend working on history."

A sudden thought hit me then. "Maybe we should work over at your house."

Vanessa wrinkled up her nose. "But you've got all the books and everything here."

"It's just three books, Vanessa. Maybe it would be easier to work someplace where there isn't a dance studio."

Vanessa giggled. "I guess so," she said. "I'll ask my mom. I'll call you. Well, bye!" And she ran out into the twilight.

I went upstairs and pressed a cold washcloth on my eyes. A little while later Mom called us for dinner. She'd fixed my favorite—spaghetti with tomato sauce.

"Well, Patti-cakes," said Dad when we were sitting down at the table. "I heard what happened at cheerleading practice."

"Is Patti going to get punished?" asked Missy.

"Being suspended is punishment enough," Mom said softly.

I started to cry again.

"A suspension isn't the worse thing in the world," Dad said.

I glanced up at him. "How can you say that?"

"Because it's true. A suspension will give you a little time to think things over."

Tears plopped onto my spaghetti.

"Let's talk about this later, Bill," Mom said.

"Just one more thing, while we're on the subject." He darted a look at Mom. "I happen to know some very fine people who have been suspended."

"Who?" asked Missy. "Snake-eye?"

"No, not Snake-eye." Dad chuckled. "Or even Uncle Charlie. A much closer relative."

"Bill!" Mom exclaimed. "You're not going to tell the children that awful story!"

"Yes!" cried Missy. "Yes! Tell us the awful story!"

Dad grinned. "Hold up your right hands and promise never to tell." And when we did, he said, "It was me."

"You?" I couldn't believe it. "What from?"

"From the University of Texas football team," he said.

"It was his freshman year," Mom said. "Before he met me."

"Five other players and I did something really stupid."

"What?" said Missy.

"We were a pretty strong bunch of young men," Dad said. "And we had one teacher who gave all the football players a hard time in his class. One night we saw his car—a green Honda—parked on the street. We decided it would be funny to play a trick on him."

"What did you do?" asked Missy.

"We picked up his car," Dad said. "And we carried it over to the football field. We set it down right on the fifty-yard line."

Missy started laughing. Mom tried to look disapproving.

"The teacher reported his car stolen. The police began looking for it. We caused a lot of trouble for a lot of people."

Dad pressed his lips together and shook his head.

"To make a long story short," he went on, "the six of us got suspended from the team for two weeks. Some of those boys were pretty fine players, too. That next weekend U. T. had a game against Arkansas, and we *lost!* We all felt bad. We'd let our team down. That was the worst part of it."

"What about that teacher?" asked Missy. "Was he mad at you?"

Dad nodded. "We had to work for him to pay for what we'd done. The first thing he did was make us wash his car. You know what he gave us to clean the hub caps? A toothbrush!"

"Served you right, too!" Mom declared.

"Yes, it did," Dad agreed. "It surely did." He turned to me. "Being suspended from the team gave me plenty to think about. Just like this suspension is going to give you, Patti-cakes."

I nodded. While Dad told his story, I'd tried to eat my spaghetti. But most of it still sat there in the bowl. I knew I couldn't eat another bite. I was worried. What if I never felt like eating again? How would I ever get back onto the squad?

Just then the doorbell rang.

"Who in the world can that be?" Mom said, getting up.

I heard voices. Suddenly Lauren and Tara walked into our dining room. I squeezed my eyes shut. I tried my hardest not to start crying again.

"Have you girls eaten supper?" Mom asked.

"Yes, Mrs. Richardson," Lauren said. "Thank you."

"Well, Patti's finished, too. Why don't you all go on

into the studio?" Mom said. "I'll bring in some dessert."

I led the way. Inside, I turned the lights to dim. The darker the better for my poor, bloodshot eyes.

"Kill 'em!" cried Petey as I sat down near his cage.

This made us all laugh a little bit. Lauren sat down beside me. Tara sat opposite us.

"Tara," I said, "you told Beth Ann I'd been dieting!"

"You're right," said Tara. "I did."

"Me, too," Lauren said. "We're all scared for you, Patti."

Tears were running down my cheeks now. "I just can't believe I'm suspended from cheerleading!"

"What did Beth Ann say?" asked Lauren. "What do you have to do to get back on the squad?"

"Eat," I said. "I have to get back to one-hundred pounds."

"Well, that shouldn't be too hard!" Tara exclaimed.

I just shrugged. I wanted to be back on the squad so much! But the thought of eating a lot, of gaining weight, was scary.

"Patti," Lauren said, "you and Tara and Cassie and I have been friends since before school started this year, right?"

I nodded.

"We're a team," she went on. "Remember when Tara got mad and ran out of here before cheerleading tryouts? The three of us went over to her apartment and talked her out of quitting."

"Remember when Cassie flipped over losing the

election?" Tara put in. "We cut practice and went over to her house."

"Yeah." I smiled through my tears. "We ran the whole way."

"It was miles!" Lauren exclaimed. "But here's the thing. When one of us is in trouble, we're all in trouble together."

"So you think I'm in trouble?" I said, sniffing.

"I do," said Lauren. "You've lost so much weight. And you just don't seem like yourself anymore."

"People change," I sniffed. "I sort of wanted to change. But . . ." I shrugged. "It got all mixed up. Anyway, if the four of us are supposed to be a team, where's Cassie?"

Tara and Lauren glanced at each other. "She's pretty upset about what happened," Lauren said. "About falling."

"Again," said Tara.

"Oh, right!" I covered my mouth with my hand. Cassie had been on Kelsey's shoulders when Kelsey fell and broke her ankle.

Tara stifled a giggle. "I'm sorry," she said. "It's not funny. Really it isn't. It's just that Cassie's so *mad!*"

Lauren started giggling, too. "She was stomping around the gym, yelling that she won't *ever* be a flyer again in her life!"

I couldn't help myself. Through my tears I joined in the laughing. "I'm glad Cassie wasn't hurt," I said. "But she could have been. And it would have been my fault."

"She'll get over it," Lauren said. "Falls are part of cheerleading."

Mom brought in a big platter of fresh fruit then. She also handed me the cordless phone. "For you," she said.

"Hello?" I mouthed to Lauren and Tara: "It's Cassie!"

Cassie gave me a major scolding. I couldn't get a word in edgewise. I tried to tell her how sorry I was that I'd dropped her. But she wouldn't stop talking for a second.

Finally Tara grabbed the phone. "Cassie, clam up!" she said. "Patti has something to say to you."

I took the phone back. "Cass? Listen, I'm really sorry. Really. No, it won't. Never. Okay, you don't have to. Not ever. There are plenty of bases you can work with on the squad."

Cassie squawked for a little while longer. Then she calmed down. At last she said, "I wish I were over there with you guys."

"I wish you were here, too." I glanced up through the skylight. The sky was thick with stars. "It's really nice here in the studio—hold it! I mean here in the *cartwheel room.*"

Lauren and Tara both jumped to their feet when I said that. They started whooping and clapping. Then they each started turning cartwheels. Too many cartwheels to count.

CHAPTER 15

The next day at school I tried not to look at the bulletin boards in the hallways. They were covered with good-luck messages for all the girls on the basketball team.

"Good luck, Liza! Power to the Tower!"

"Here's to Jade! The Jewel of our Team!"

At lunchtime the boys' basketball team held a pep rally for the girls' team. I tried to cheer along. Was it ever hard!

I had mixed feelings about seeing Vanessa. On the one hand, I was mad at her. She had *not* been sympathetic about my big crisis. Yet in a way, it would be good to see her. At least she wouldn't talk about basketball or cheerleading.

But when I got to history class, Vanessa wasn't there.

"Well, have you two about wrapped up your work on King George?" Mr. Noonan asked as I sat by myself working on our report.

"Pretty much," I said. But I hadn't finished writing my half of the report. Had Vanessa even *started* on hers? I didn't know.

"I'd like you girls to give your report first on Monday." Mr. Noonan smiled. "I want to inspire the other students."

"Oh, okay," I said. "We'll go first."

Mr. Noonan walked over to Emily's desk then. I was worried. Today was already Thursday. If I really worked all weekend, I'd be ready on Monday. But what about Vanessa?

That night I worked for hours on the report. I also kept calling Vanessa. But her answering machine just kept picking up. *Hi! This is Vanessa!* it said. *When you hear the beep, do a grand jeté and leave your message!*

I hung up every time.

On Friday morning, I slowly put on a pair of dark red jeans and a white cotton sweater. It was the first Friday all year that I wasn't wearing my cheerleading uniform.

"You and Daddy and Missy go to the game," I told Mom at breakfast. "I don't want you to miss it."

"Oh, honey," Mom said. "Your daddy and I have seen enough basketball games to last us a lifetime. It won't bother us a bit to miss this one!"

I put my arms around Mom and gave her a hug. I knew she wasn't exactly telling the truth. But it made me feel better anyway.

Friday was the worst day of my life. Just about everyone was wearing the school colors. At lunch there was a spirit parade. To top it off, Vanessa was absent in history class again. Now I was *really* worried.

Mom picked me up right after school. We dropped Missy off at Tiffany's house, where she was having a sleepover.

"Mom, I'm afraid something terrible's happened to Vanessa," I said when Missy had gotten out of the van.

"What makes you think so?"

"She wasn't at school again today. Last night I couldn't reach her on the phone. Something's wrong. And it must be an emergency. Or she would have told me she wouldn't be in school."

"Well, keep trying to call her," Mom said.

"I wonder if her grandfather's sick," I said. "Maybe he's in the hospital or something."

Mom pulled up in front of our house. "I'm going over to Fran Jacobs's, honey. She's having a little meeting for some of the aerobics instructors in the area."

"Okay," I said.

"I'll be home around six. If you haven't reached Vanessa by then, we'll sit down and figure out what to do."

I was too upset to work on the report. For nearly an hour I called Vanessa. But all I got was her machine.

Then I pulled out the phone book. I knew Vanessa's number wasn't listed. But maybe hei parents number was. There was just one Ivanova in the book: Alexander. And there was his number! Quickly I dialed it.

But all I got was another recording. This number, it said, had been disconnected.

I checked the address. It was 320 Shore Road.

Seeing the address gave me another idea. I found our big yellow book map. It showed every single street in and around Paxton. I checked the index and found Shore Road. *That's funny,* I thought. It wasn't on the far side of the lake at all. It was on the near side—really close to my house!

The kitchen clock said four o'clock. I scribbled a quick note and put it on the kitchen counter. Then I ran to the garage and took out my bike. I was on my way to Vanessa's!

I felt nervous as I rode. What would I say to Vanessa's elegant mother if she answered the door? Or to her handsome-as-a-movie-star father? What if her grandfather was really sick? What if he was dying? Then a really awful thought struck me. Vanessa's ancestors had such terrible things happen to them. What if Vanessa's family had been in some disaster? What if their furnace had exploded? What if her whole family had been blown to bits? What if . . .

I made myself stop thinking *what ifs.* Somehow I kept riding. It took me less than five minutes to reach Shore Road. I watched the numbers go up from the 100s to the 200s. The houses along Shore Road were pretty average looking. Along the sidewalk little kids were riding bikes with training wheels. Moms were pushing strollers toward the lake. I thought the houses would get bigger and fancier as the address numbers rose. But they didn't. They stayed ordinary. Suddenly, there on my right, was 320.

I put on my brakes. It wasn't exactly what I'd been expecting. It was a small one-story house with dark shingles.

My heart began to beat fast. Maybe I was at the wrong place. Maybe I should turn my bike around and ride home. I almost did. But then I saw something lettered on the mailbox: A. IVANOVA, TAI—. The rest of the name had been scratched out. But this had to be Vanessa's house. It had to! And I had to find out what was going on.

It was a sunny, blue-skied April afternoon. There were dozens of kids playing ball and flying kites in nearby yards. Yet as I walked up that sidewalk, my heart pounded as if I were entering a haunted mansion. I propped my bike against a tree. I drew a deep breath. I stabbed my finger at the doorbell.

I heard it buzzing inside the house. Then I heard footsteps. Someone was coming! Slowly the door creaked open. A bearded man stood before me. He had to be Vanessa's grandfather. He looked a lot older than my Grandma Ellie. A worn yellow tape measure hung around his neck. He didn't say anything.

"Hello," I made myself say. "I'm Patti. I'm looking for Vanessa."

Now his stern expression melted into a smile. "Vanessa!" he said, nodding. "Vanessa no here."

"Oh, she's not? Well, do you know when she'll be back?"

"Vanessa no here," he repeated. He opened the

door wider then. He made a gesture with his hand. He seemed to be asking me to come in and see for myself that Vanessa wasn't home.

I shook my head. "No, thank you," I said. Then I added very slowly, "When will Vanessa come home?"

"Ah, Vanessa," he said, nodding.

I looked beyond him then, into the house. What I saw looked more like a workroom than a living room. Bolts of fabric were piled high on a wide table. The table was littered with pattern pieces, scraps of material, pinking shears. A rack of clothes with notes pinned on them stood in one corner of the room. Next to it was a sewing machine. On the machine lay a piece of blue velvet.

I'd found Vanessa's dressmaker. Her very own grandfather. A. Ivanova, tailor. I'd discovered one more of Vanessa's secrets.

"Thank you, Mr. Ivanova," I said. A phone began to ring inside the house. The man made no move to answer it.

I turned to go then. The man stayed in the doorway. I heard a high-pitched voice say, *Hi! This is Vanessa! When you hear the beep, do a grand jeté and leave your message!*

I hopped on my bike. I rode home with my head spinning.

CHAPTER 16

"It *was* Vanessa's house," I told my parents at dinner that night. I was too upset to eat. "But she told me she lived in a huge house, a palace. Why would she lie to me?"

Mom glanced at Dad. "Vanessa has a pretty strong imagination," she said.

"Maybe sometimes she has trouble telling where real life ends," Dad added. "And one of her fairy tales begins."

"But where *is* Vanessa?" I said. "She's disappeared! I don't know what to do about her part of the history report."

When I was excused, I hurried up to my room. I turned the radio to the station that broadcast local sports. But they had on the Riverview versus Clayton *boys'* basketball game. Didn't they know that Paxton versus Hazelwood *girls'* basketball was the big game in town?

I looked through magazines for a while. Then I put

some new pictures on my bulletin board. Finally I took *The Letters of Nicholas and George* from my desk and sat with it on my bed. I'd been foolish to wait for Vanessa to put my report together. Now I started taking more notes.

The phone rang around nine-thirty. It had to be Vanessa! I picked it up.

"Patti? It's me, Lauren. How're you doing? Are you okay?"

I let out my breath. "I'm okay. What happened? Did we win?"

"Eighty-five to fifty-four."

"Yippee!" I cried quickly, getting into the spirit. "All right, Paxton!"

"The Regionals are next weekend! And, Patti? Come over tomorrow morning, okay? Gram'll make you a big stack of pancakes. They'll fatten you up in no time!"

But the thought of buttery, syrupy pancakes made me shudder.

"Thanks anyway, Lauren," I said. "But I'm spending every minute this weekend working on my report."

"What? You haven't finished it yet?" she asked. "It seems like every time I've talked to you lately, Vanessa was coming over so you could work on that thing."

"Well, Vanessa came over," I said. "But we never really got down to work." I sighed. We talked some more and then hung up.

I was sorry to miss breakfast at Lauren's. But for three weeks, I'd hardly eaten any fat at all. No way could I start right off with butter-soaked pancakes! And my feelings about it frightened me. What if I *couldn't* gain weight?

Then I remembered the game! I raced out of my room to tell everybody the good news. My parents' bedroom door was closed. But Missy's light was still on. Well, at least I could tell her. I ran down the hall. At her doorway I stopped. Missy was sprawled out on her bed, sound asleep. Granny Nelly's quilt was rumpled at her feet. I tugged at the quilt, pulling it up. I tucked it around my sister. The worn coverlet felt soft in my hands. I sat down on Missy's bed for the first time. I studied the quilt's interlocking circles. A wedding ring pattern, Mom had called it. I looked at a little blue-and-white checked square. Next to it was a square with tiny pink flowers. I noticed that not every square was checkered gingham. There were polka dots, stripes, and geometric designs. All were in delicate patterns. All had been stitched together by Granny Nelly's hands.

I smoothed the quilt over Missy. Her cheek, I saw, was resting on a little notebook. A pencil lay between her fingers.

I slid the pencil out of her hand. I picked up her head and pulled the little book out. What was it, anyway?

Then I saw what it was. On the cover of the little notebook, Missy had printed three words: *My Fat Book.*

"Oh, no!" I breathed. Frightened, I flipped up the cover. In big printed letters, with wild misspellings,

Missy had written down what she'd had to eat every day. At the bottom of the page was her weight: sixty-five pounds. I flipped the pages. Her weight went down to sixty-three. Then sixty-one. I turned to the last page. She was down to sixty! My little sister had lost six pounds!

"Missy?" Gently I shook her shoulder. "Missy? Wake up!"

"Huh?" mumbled Missy. She opened her eyes, squinting in the bright light of her room. "What's the matter, Patti?"

I got up and turned off the overhead light. "Guess what? Paxton won the basketball game!"

"Oh." Missy closed her eyes again. "Yippee."

"Let's celebrate," I said. "How would you like to come down to the kitchen? We'll have a midnight snack!"

"Is it midnight?" she asked, opening her eyes again.

"Close enough," I said. "Come on."

I wrapped the quilt around Missy's shoulders, and we went down the stairs. In the kitchen I turned on just one low light to keep a midnight mood. I filled the kettle and put it on a burner. Then I got out the cocoa mix.

"Are we having hot chocolate?" asked Missy.

"With the works," I said as I took a bag of tiny marshmallows from a high shelf.

"But doesn't hot chocolate have fat in it?" asked Missy.

"Yep," I said. "But it's so boring always worrying about fat. Don't you think?"

"Yes!" said Missy. "And besides, hot chocolate tastes good."

I poured boiling water into our mugs and stirred to mix it with the chocolate. I put three mini-marshmallows in my cup. But I put lots in Missy's. I added a bit of milk, too, to cool it off. I put out a plate of cookies.

"Wow! This is a fat feast!" Missy exclaimed. She sat down and reached for a cookie.

"Speaking of fat," I said. "I saw your Fat Book."

"It's just like yours," Missy said with her mouth half full. "Just like yours and Vanessa's."

I nodded. "But you know something? I'm not keeping a Fat Book any more. It's not a very good idea."

"It isn't?" Missy said.

I shook my head. "It's not good to lose too much weight."

"But you've been losing weight, Patti. I saw how the numbers went down and down in your Fat Book."

I nodded. "That was stupid of me, Missy. I wasn't just dieting. I was practically starving myself. That's dangerous. That's what got me kicked off the squad. I'm not doing it anymore."

"I hope I won't get kicked off my squad," said Missy.

"You won't," I said. "But you've got to start eating again, Missy. I saw the numbers in your book, too. You've lost so much weight!" Tears stung my eyes as I spoke.

"Um, Patti?"

"Hmm?"

"Don't worry about how many pounds I lost. Okay?"

"But I am worried!" I told her. "It's not good at all!"

"But I didn't really lose them, Patti."

"You didn't?"

Missy shook her blond curls.

"I just kept weighing the same thing every day," she said. "So I made up numbers. I made them go down and down. Just like your numbers."

"Oh, Missy!" I leaped up and hugged my sister. Tears spilled down my cheeks. "That's the best made-up thing I've ever heard!"

I caught my breath and blew my nose. Then I took a teeny sip of my hot chocolate. To my relief, it tasted really good.

"Mmmm!" I said.

"Mmmm!" Missy said back.

I took a bigger sip. And then another. As I drank my cocoa, my worries about food and eating began to fade. It might take a while for me to work up to Lauren's Gram's pancakes. But I'd get there.

My sister and I sat at our kitchen table, talking and snacking, for a long time. We talked about the old times in Texas. And about seeing our first snowfall in Paxton. Then Missy told me all about how Tiffany liked to give her Barbie dolls haircuts. And how she was teaching Spooky to hold up his front paw when she said, "Shake!"

Suddenly I noticed Mom standing in the doorway. "Is this a private party?" she asked. "Or can anybody come?"

"Paxton won the basketball game," Missy told her. "We're celebrating."

Mom rubbed the top of Missy's head.

I put the kettle on again, and Mom joined us for another round of hot cocoa and cookies.

"Well, Patti, honey," said Mom, pushing her chair back from the table. "Can I take this little party as a sign that your sanity about eating has returned?"

"You can." I smiled. "Right, Missy?"

"What's sanity?" asked Missy.

"It means the opposite of crazy," Mom told her. "And crazy is how Patti was getting about food."

"But can I tell you something, Mom?" I said. "Tonight's a celebration. I'm not going to have cocoa and cookies every night. And I don't want to go back to eating things with tons of fat. Things like mashed potatoes with cream."

"Can I tell you something, Patrice?" Mom said. "I know a thing or two about a healthful diet. For your information, I make my mashed potatoes with skimmed milk."

"You do?" I gave her a suspicious look. "Then why does Daddy always call them 'Sunny's famous creamy mashed potatoes'?"

Mom burst out laughing. "Because there aren't any lumps in them, silly!"

"Oh," I said, laughing, too. "That kind of creamy."

"Listen, honey, I know what I'm doing," she said. "Let's just enjoy our meals and have fun eating together as a family. Let's stop all the fuss about fat and calories."

"Okay," I said. "I'll stop."

"And we'll all live happily ever after," said Missy. "Now can we go to bed?"

Missy went up to her room. But Mom and I sat at the table for a while. We talked, too. Mom even told me a story about Granny Nelly riding horseback all through the night to get some medicine for her husband, Dan.

"Cool," I said when she was finished. "How come you never told me that story before?"

"I just didn't think about it, honey," Mom said.

"I like hearing stories about my ancestors," I said.

"Well, when I talk to Grandma Ellie tomorrow, I'll ask her to remind me of some more stories." She patted my hand. "But I hope you won't be disappointed if none of your ancestors turn out to have royal blood in their veins."

"No, that's okay," I told her. "Texas blood is good enough for me."

Saturday morning I woke up in a panic. The history report! I didn't know what to do about it. I called Vanessa. But when her machine answered, I hung up. I decided to go to Madame Federova's. I didn't feel like taking class. But there was no way Vanessa would miss *her* class. I had to see her. I had to talk to her.

I rode my bike into Paxton. I arrived at Madame's just before ten. I checked the sign-in sheet. Vanessa's name wasn't there.

I looked for her in the dressing room anyway. I looked everywhere I could think of. Okay, she might skip the ten o'clock class. But I couldn't imagine her missing her eleven o'clock class. So I sat down in the lobby and waited. At two minutes to eleven, she still wasn't there.

At eleven Madame dismissed the ten o'clock class. I poked my head into the studio. The advanced dancers were lacing up their toe shoes.

"Excuse me," I said to a girl in a white leotard. I'd seen Vanessa talking to her. "Have you seen Vanessa today?"

"She's not here," the girls said. "She's in New York."

"New York?"

"Yes," said the girl. "Didn't you know? She's auditioning for the School of American Ballet."

CHAPTER 17

Patti!" Vanessa ran up to me on Monday when I walked into history class. Her eyes were shining. "Guess what?"

"You got into the School of American Ballet," I said.

"Yes!" she squealed. She grabbed my arm. "I made it! I'm in!" Holding my arm as if it were a barre, she did a little spin. "We're moving to New York!"

"Congratulations," I said.

"Thank you! Oh, I'm so excited! I'm starting in the summer program! It's just two months away!"

"Vanessa?" I said.

She stopped spinning. "What?"

"How come you didn't tell me that you were going to New York for the audition?" I asked. "I was really worried about you."

She pressed her lips together. Then she whispered, "I'm superstitious. I wanted to keep it a secret. I thought it would bring me good luck."

"So how come a girl in the eleven o'clock class at the ballet studio knew?" I said.

Vanessa frowned slightly. "Well, Madame knew," she said. "She's been helping me get ready for the audition for months. Maybe she told some of the girls in the advanced class. I don't know."

"Can we come to order now?" Mr. Noonan called. We took our seats. "Well, today's the day," he continued. "Today we'll begin hearing your oral reports on Russian history."

Vanessa stared at me. She mouthed, "Yuck!"

I just looked away.

"I'd like to get this project off to an inspiring start," Mr. Noonan went on. "So I've asked Vanessa Ivanova and Patti Richardson to present their report first. Girls?"

I stood up. "I'll give the first part of the report." I walked to the front of the classroom carrying my paper. My paper that I'd spent so many weeks trying to start. My paper that I'd spent *all* of Saturday and Sunday finishing.

"The future King George the Fifth was born in England about the same time that the future Tsar Nicholas was born in Russia," I began.

I told how George and Nicholas were first cousins. I talked about how, when they were young, Georgie, as he was called, and Nicky were good friends. I told stories that I'd read in the letters they wrote to each other.

"One day Tsar Nicholas would need King George to save his life. And to save the lives of his wife and children," I said at the end of my report. "No one would have suspected what George would do."

"Yes!" Mr. Noonan exclaimed. "Very nice, Patti. Very nice indeed. This is just the kind of story—about real people and their real suffering—that . . ." Half the class chanted with him as he said, "puts meat on the bones of history!"

Everybody laughed. Even Mr. Noonan.

"Well," he said, "let's not leave the story hanging there. Vanessa?"

Vanessa walked to the front of the room. She had no notes. No paper. But that didn't stop her from talking. I had to hand it to her. She remembered every little snippet of the reading that I'd told her about. Plus she knew a lot of Russian history. She wove it all into her report. She told stories of what life was like for wealthy people in Russia before the revolution. She told of gilded coaches drawn by white horses. About skating on frozen ponds, tobogganing on hills of ice, suppers of caviar and little pancakes called blinis.

She talked on and on. But she seemed to forget that she was supposed to be doing a report about King George and Nicholas.

"And I guess that's all," said Vanessa at last. She gave Mr. Noonan her most brilliant smile.

"Vanessa," said Mr. Noonan, "your report was full of fascinating details about the lives of your colorful ancestors."

"Thank you," said Vanessa, still smiling.

"However," Mr. Noonan went on, "it was rather

lean on historical facts about King George." He peered at her for a moment. Then he wrotc something in his grade book.

Zena and Emily were next. They told us all about the mad monk, Gregory Rasputin. They showed us lots of photographs of him, too. Was he ever gross! He never bathed or combed his hair or beard. Yet he ruled Russia, as Zena said, "from behind the throne." When Emily told about his gruesome death—he was poisoned, shot, *and* drowned—all the boys started clapping!

By the time Zena and Emily finished, Mr. Noonan was practically dizzy with joy. "All right, class dismissed," he said at last. "Those who gave your reports today, see me before you go."

Zena and Emily zoomed up to Mr. Noonan's desk. He didn't even try to hide their grades: A plus and A plus. So their combined grade was—guess what?—A plus!

When Emily and Zena left, he turned the grade book toward me. Hey! I'd gotten an A minus!

"The minus because you had no visual aides," he said.

Then he turned the book to Vanessa. Her grade was a C minus. "And I was generous," he told her. "Your combined grade is a B minus."

As I gathered up my books, I felt my face growing warmer and warmer. Vanessa was already walking out the door. Part of me wanted to let her go. But another part of me wanted to talk to Vanessa. That part won.

"Vanessa!" I ran into the hallway. "Wait a second!"

She turned and I caught up with her. "You didn't

work on our report at all!" I said angrily. "You knew we'd be graded together. Now half of *my* grade is your lousy C minus!"

"Well, how was I supposed to do any reading?" said Vanessa. "I mean, you hogged those books the whole time!"

"That's a lie!" I said. "And you know it!"

"Oh, so what?" She began tapping her fingers impatiently on her notebook.

"So what?" I said. "You just lie whenever you feel like it, don't you? You're a big fat liar!"

"I'm not a big *fat* anything!" Vanessa made a face.

"That reminds me," I said, digging in my backpack. "Here." I handed back her copy of *Fat-free Eating.* "Missy had it," I told her. "She'd started keeping a Fat Book like we were."

"Oh, cool," said Vanessa.

"It *isn't* cool," I said. "It's sick! Missy's a little kid. She thought you were so great. She wanted to be just like you."

"Well, who wouldn't?" said Vanessa.

Was she joking? I couldn't tell.

"I . . . I just want to say . . ." I began. What did I want to say? "I thought we were friends, but . . ."

"We are!" Vanessa flashed me a smile.

I shook my head. "Friends don't treat each other the way you treated me. You only pretended to like me so you could use our studio," I said. "Our *cartwheel room.* All you wanted was to practice for your big audition."

Vanessa shrugged. "I had to practice," she said.

"But why didn't you just tell me that?" I said.

"I didn't want to talk about the audition," she said. "Because then, if I didn't make it . . ." Her voice trailed off.

"So you just disappeared," I said. "You packed up all your tapes and CDs that were at our house and went off to New York. Didn't you think that I might wonder where you were? That I might be worried?"

"Not really."

"Well, I was! I must have called your number a hundred times. I thought something awful had happened to you! I even rode my bike over to your house to see if you were okay."

Vanessa narrowed her eyes. "You don't know where I live."

"Yes, I do, Vanessa. Three-twenty Shore Road."

"No," said Vanessa. "That's my . . . my uncle's house."

"No," I said. "That's your house. But so what if it's not a palace? It doesn't matter. Don't you know that?"

For a moment Vanessa just looked at me. Then she said, "I have to go to ballet."

"Bye, Vanessa," I said.

I felt sad watching Vanessa hurry off, her huge ballet bag bouncing at her side. She didn't seem so elegant anymore. Her own private world was a fantasy. And not one of her little secrets turned out to be worth knowing.

I wasn't fooled by Vanessa any longer. But still, I'd miss her. I'd had so much fun with her. Or . . . had I?

I walked slowly down the hall, thinking. Working on the report with her hadn't been any fun. Not at all. Talking with Vanessa? That had been mostly Vanessa—talking about Vanessa. And the dancing? That, too, was all Vanessa. In her mind she was the Rose Princess. I was the Daisy Princess, content to stand on the sidelines. Remembering that made me mad! I'd stood there, watching her. I'd just stood there, with my head tilted until my neck was totally stiff. Come to think of it, hanging around with Vanessa had been mostly a pain in the neck!

"Beth Ann?" I said as I walked into the gym. "If you've got a minute to come down to the nurse's office with me, I think you can put me back on the squad."

Beth Ann smiled. "Let's go!"

I stepped onto the scale. It hit 100, right on the mark.

"You don't have rocks in your pockets or anything, do you?" she teased me.

"Nope, it's all me," I said. "One-hundred percent Patti Richardson."

As I said that, I thought it sounded pretty good. That's exactly who I wanted to be. Which didn't mean that I was exactly the same as before. I wasn't. But from now on, any changing I did would be because it was right for me. And not because I was copying somebody else.

Beth Ann and I walked back to the gym then. We got there in the middle of a little birthday celebration for Susan Delgado.

"You missed the singing," Tara told me. She put

an arm around my shoulder. "But you're just in time for the eats."

Heather Smyth and Joannie Nichols were passing out cupcakes.

"Here you go, Patti," Joannie said, holding out the cupcake box.

"Thanks!" I said, taking a small one. "Yum, chocolate."

Cassie and Lauren jogged over to where Tara and I were standing.

"Patti, you're back!" said Lauren. "I'm so happy!"

"Yeah, me, too," I said.

"Listen, Patti," said Cassie. "By next week I might be ready to do a stunt with you. I'm not promising anything. But maybe."

"Thanks, Cassie!" I said, laughing.

"Now, Patti," Tara said, "you and I have something really, *really* serious to talk to you about."

"I know," I said. "I'm sorry I didn't listen when you told me Vanessa wasn't a real friend. She wasn't. But you are."

"That's nice," said Tara briskly. "But what we really have to talk about are those new shoes of yours. See, I'm going to Chicago this weekend, and Dad's taking us to this big party at—"

"Tara?" I interrupted her. "The shoes are yours."

"Great! When can I borrow them?"

"You can have them," I said. "For keeps. They're not my style."

"Oh, Patti!" Tara said. "Oh, man! Those shoes are going to look so hot with my new black fringed skirt!"

She looked so funny then, jumping for joy, her baby barrettes bouncing around on her head.

As for my New Me outfit, I couldn't imagine wearing it again, either. The cotton sweater would look okay with a pair of jeans. But the skirt? I knew the perfect place for it—Missy's dress-up bin!

"Okay, cheerleaders!" Beth Ann called. "Let's stretch out!"

I hit the mat with Tara, Cassie, and Lauren. We all started stretching out. All of us, together.